P9-DOF-647

# LORD AND LADY BUNNY—
## ALMOST ROYALTY!

DISCARD

# LORD AND LADY BUNNY- ALMOST ROYALTY!

### BY MR. & MRS. BUNNY

*translated from the Rabbit by*
POLLY HORVATH

*illustrated by*
SOPHIE BLACKALL

schwartz & wade books · new york

This is a work of fiction. Names, characters, places, and incidents either are the product of the author's imagination or are used fictitiously. Any resemblance to actual persons, living or dead, events, or locales is entirely coincidental.

Text copyright © 2014 by Polly Horvath
Jacket art and interior illustrations copyright © 2014 by Sophie Blackall

All rights reserved. Published in the United States by Schwartz & Wade Books,
an imprint of Random House Children's Books,
a division of Random House, Inc., New York.

Schwartz & Wade Books and the colophon are trademarks of Random House, Inc.

Visit us on the Web! randomhouse.com/kids

Educators and librarians, for a variety of teaching tools, visit us at
RHTeachersLibrarians.com

*Library of Congress Cataloging-in-Publication Data*
Horvath, Polly.
Lord and Lady Bunny—almost royalty! / by Mrs. Bunny ; translated from the
Rabbit by Polly Horvath ; illustrated by Sophie Blackall.—1st ed.
p.   cm.
Summary: "Madeleine and her hippie parents travel to England to run a candy
shop. Meanwhile Mr. and Mrs. Bunny also travel to England, where Mrs. Bunny
tries to weasel her way into the ranks of royalty."—Provided by publisher.
ISBN 978-0-307-98065-6 (hc)—ISBN 978-0-307-98066-3 (glb)—
ISBN 978-0-307-98067-0 (ebook)
[1. Human-animal communication—Fiction. 2. Hippies—Fiction. 3. Rabbits—
Fiction. 4. Voyages and travels—Fiction. 5. Kings, queens, rulers, etc.—Fiction.
6. England—Fiction.] I. Blackall, Sophie, ill. II. Title.
PZ7.H79224Lo 2014
[Fic]—dc23
2012027442

The text of this book is set in 12-point Schneidler BT.
The illustrations were rendered in ink.
Book design by Rachael Cole

Printed in the United States of America

10 9 8 7 6 5 4 3 2 1

First Edition

Random House Children's Books supports the First Amendment
and celebrates the right to read.

R0440915841

To Ken Setterington. So brilliant a human that Mrs. Bunny
suspects him of secretly being a rabbit in disguise.
—Mrs. Bunny

To Shecky Bunny—comic genius!
—Mr. Bunny

# ✿❦ CONTENTS ❦✿

The Pop-Tarts Arrive       1

Mrs. Bunny Has an Idea       17

Flo Finds His Calling       29

Mrs. Bunny's Long-Standing Dream       39

Bon Voyage       50

Shipboard Bunnies       60

Mildred Suffers a Sea Change       74

Land Ho!       98

Stranded!       113

Unstranded!       126

The Sweet Shoppe       145

The Asparagus Contretemps       167

A Surprise for Mrs. Bunny       180

Mr. Bunny Makes Some Friends       198

Mrs. Bunny's Big Day       215

Training the Candy       235

Tea with . . . . . . . . . THE QUEEEEEEN!!!!!       254

Mrs. Bunny Is Finally Crowned       270

# ◄THE POP-TARTS ARRIVE►

It was summer on Hornby Island.

This was good and bad.

The good part was that the island was warm and lovely. Fragrant with pine and flower blossoms, the seabeds full of sand dollars, the meadows full of deer. Madeline noticed a new fawn who grazed by her bedroom window every morning. She would awaken to its munching and peek out the screen, careful not to startle it. She could hear the sweet chirping of all the birds at sunrise and the gentle croaking of the tree frogs lulling her to sleep at sunset.

The bad part was that the island population tripled as tourists flocked to camp on Hornby's one small overcrowded campground. All the roads and paths and byways were littered with people in Bermuda shorts dropping candy wrappers. It was good for business at the café where Madeline waitressed, but other than that, she had to admit, it was pretty awful.

Madeline's parents, Flo and Mildred, were particularly annoyed by the tourists. Flo's and Mildred's real names were Harry and Denise, but they asked to be called Flo and Mildred by everyone, including Madeline. They were ex-hippies who had migrated to Canada from California many years before Madeline was born. On Hornby they had their dream existence, living off the land with a little help from Mildred's sand-dollar art, the occasional marimba gig and Madeline's waitressing. The summer tourists brought Mildred more business as well, but, said Flo, at what cost?

"Why don't they all go somewhere else?" asked Flo as he and Mildred and Madeline sat down to a dinner of wild salad greens, tofu and mung bean bread.

"Why don't *we*?" asked Mildred.

Flo looked at Mildred. His mouth fell open. "Hey, why not?" he said finally. "Sometimes, Denise, I think you're a genius."

"Call me Mildred," said Mildred.

"But where can we go?" asked Flo. "I've got, like, six dollars. You?"

Mildred got out her change purse. "Twenty-seven cents."

"How much have you got, Madeline?" asked Flo.

"Two hundred and thirteen dollars. But it's in a bank."

"A *bank*?" said Flo, startled. "Bertolt Brecht said—"

"Yes, I know. What is the crime of robbing a bank compared with the crime of founding one. But I'm saving for college," said Madeline imperturbably.

"Wow. That's, like, so, you know . . ."

"Foresighted?" said Madeline.

"More like weird. You want *more* school?"

Yes, thought Madeline. And a college education fund like her best friend, Katherine.

Shortly after Katherine had become Madeline's best friend, which was shortly after they first played together, they had told each other everything about their lives and marveled at the differences, including the fact that Katherine had a college education fund and Madeline did not.

Before meeting Katherine, Madeline had never even heard of a college education fund. But ever since she had, Madeline walked around with a haunted look. She desperately wanted to go to college. Harvard would be her first choice. Madeline loved school. She loved everything about it, from its first-day-in-the-fall freshness to its end-of-the-year festivities. She loved books. She loved studying. She wanted a way to stay in school all her life. Maybe as a college professor. It amazed her that it had never occurred to her that college wasn't free like public school. And you couldn't expect the money to just show up the year you enrolled. Of course, people saved for it for years ahead of time. And naturally, Flo and Mildred, who were very in-the-now believers, hadn't put aside money for her the way Katherine's parents had. And Flo and Mildred wouldn't ever take her to a bank to help her set up a fund. Madeline started to have nightmares. In all her nightmares she was fifty years old, making sand-dollar art and watching her brain rot.

"What is the matter?" Flo and Mildred would say when she woke up screaming.

"I am watching my brain rot," she would say.

"Cool," Flo would reply.

"What is the matter?" Flo and Mildred would ask when they came upon her sitting on the porch staring fearfully into a future she wanted but couldn't afford and couldn't figure out a way to afford.

"I am penniless, and the brain? Still rotting," she would reply.

"Cool," Flo would say.

But when Katherine's mother found Madeline sitting with Katherine on the kitchen floor with a haunted expression and asked her what was wrong, and Madeline held up her two hundred dollars, saying she needed a bank account and why, Katherine's mother trotted her right down to the Canadian Imperial Bank of Commerce and helped her open a savings account. Katherine's mother had Madeline's undying gratitude, but Madeline still worried. She didn't think she could ever fill up this account with enough money for college. She made a deposit each week anyway and tried not to think about it. But this worried her too because she suspected that just not thinking about things was how Flo and Mildred had ended up on Hornby. And now they wanted to spend money they didn't have on a vacation.

Besides, she thought, she wasn't feeling particularly restless. She was still recovering from her recent adventure. At the end of her school term she had come home one day to find that her parents had been kidnapped by foxes who wanted to find out where Madeline's uncle Runyon, a government decoder, lived. Madeline had traveled to his secret location to enlist his aid, but shortly after her arrival he had fallen into a coma. She was in the depths of despair when Mr. and Mrs. Bunny had stumbled upon her. They had had twelve children of their own and were swift to come to her aid. Together they had tracked down Madeline's parents. Mrs. Bunny had even knit Madeline a pair of white shoes so that she could participate in the grade five graduation, where none other than Prince Charles gave out the awards. *And* Mr. and Mrs. Bunny had come to the graduation with her! She missed them already and had promised to visit them again this summer. She had no desire to go any farther afield than that.

"Where would you want to go if we did have enough money to leave the island?" asked Madeline, returning to the subject at hand.

"Anywhere. Egypt. That would be cool. See some hieroglyphics. You remember River Magoo?" asked Flo, turning to Mildred. "From the Haight? He went to Egypt and saw hieroglyphics and they were, like, moving, man. He was never the same."

"I didn't know River was so easily moved," said Mildred, who had always thought River was a bit of a dolt.

"No, they were, like, *moving,* dancing around the walls. River said they could, like, really shake it."

"Hieroglyphics are ancient writing on a wall," said Madeline. "They don't dance."

"Maybe not for you or me, but River tended to be in a hyperspiritual state," said Flo. "And travel opens you up. Let's go to Egypt. Let's see some of those dancing hieroglyphics."

"On six dollars and twenty-seven cents?" asked Mildred.

"Madeline's got two hundred dollars . . . ," said Flo tentatively.

"Not on your life," said Madeline crisply. "Besides, even that wouldn't be enough."

"Where can we go for six dollars and twenty-seven cents?" asked Mildred.

"McDonald's," said Flo glumly. He looked crestfallen.

Madeline had some sympathy. If she hadn't been hoping to visit the Bunnys and hadn't been so tired from her last adventure, she might have liked a vacation too. The only place she had ever been was the mainland, and that was cut short when Flo found out that The Olde Spaghetti Factory, where they were eating, wasn't serving union lettuce.

"I've finished my tofu and mung bean sandwich," said Madeline, standing up and carrying her plate to the sink.

"Want some more?" asked Flo, passing her the tofu and the mung bean bread. "We can be grateful. We may not have Paris but we'll always have the clever mung bean."

"It's nature's nutritional wonder," said Mildred.

"No thanks, I've got to hurry to get the next ferry. Katherine invited me for a sleepover. Can I stay the whole weekend?"

"Talk about, like, going someplace else," said Flo. "This is synchronicity. You're going, like, *someplace else*!"

"Did Katherine's mom *ask* you for the whole weekend?" asked Mildred.

"Go with the flow," murmured Flo. Then a thought occurred to him. "Hey, that could be, like, my motto or something."

"You guys are going to Zanky's for dinner tomorrow night anyway. And Katherine's mom says she's always glad I'm there," said Madeline.

Katherine had five brothers, all of them devoted to soccer, fastball, basketball, football and hockey. Katherine's mom spent every waking minute of every day driving someone somewhere. Katherine was the only one in the family not sports-inclined. Her mother, Mrs. Vandermeer, didn't know what to do with her. There seemed to be no place to drive her. When Katherine and Madeline formed a friendship, it was the best thing that had ever happened to Mrs. Vandermeer. Madeline kept Katherine completely entertained, so that Mrs. Vandermeer didn't have to worry about leaving her in the house undriven.

Madeline opened her knapsack to pack it for the weekend. That's when she spied the cinnamon sugar Pop-Tarts. Katherine had shoved them in there on Madeline's last visit. Madeline had forgotten about them. Mrs. Vandermeer did not allow her children to have any sugar. She was a very by-the-book mom, and she believed that sugar caused all kinds of maladies but most especially hyperactivity. There was no evidence to support this, but all of Mrs. Vandermeer's soccer-mom friends knew it to be true. The same way they knew that if they didn't drive their children to some form of entertainment or find some way to keep them occupied every second from school closing until bedtime, the children would not know what to do with themselves and would resort to staring at the wall until their heads exploded. Suburban homes were very neat, and no one wanted to be picking brain bits off the walls.

This was the same school of thought that came up with the idea that when children read books, they should summarize each chapter when they were finished with it. Nothing had done so much to kill a generation's love of reading.

Before Madeline had Katherine as a friend and got to observe suburban life up close, she had worried that Flo and Mildred would be thought eccentric by her schoolmates. But a few visits to the thick of suburban Comox, peering in on Katherine's life, and Madeline began to feel that the way she had been brought up was not so outrageous after all. What her parents were doing on Hornby was no crazier than anything anyone else was doing.

Katherine thought Madeline's life was fabulous, being left to read in a hammock all day and never pressured to join groups or go to day camps. Learning silversmithing and wearing long peasant dresses and participating in magical candlelit celebrations on the beach. Having deer grazing outside your bedroom window and growing your own food. Katherine thought Madeline had it made in the shade. But, Madeline pointed out, Katherine didn't have to worry about money, her parents worried about that for her. And her roof never leaked and mice never invaded, and her parents came to her parent-teacher conferences and graduations and school events. And she didn't have to buy her shoes at the Salvation Army. *And,* most importantly, Katherine had a college fund.

"Well, *your* mom lets you eat sugar," countered Katherine.

"If we ever have it around, which we usually don't because we can't afford it. We have beehives and my mom uses honey instead. *You* get store-bought treats."

"*Sugar-free* store-bought treats," Katherine reminded her bitterly.

The last time Madeline had been to Katherine's, they had come in on Mrs. Vandermeer having a fit in the kitchen.

"*Look* what Uncle Kevin sent us. It must have been him. Who else would send us a case of cinnamon sugar Pop-Tarts? Ever since he moved to the States, he sends us the most outrageous products. It's kindly meant, but he should know better than to send us *sugar*! It was bad enough when he sent us a case of spray cheese in a can."

Mrs. Vandermeer was pacing about her granite kitchen island, on which the Pop-Tarts sat, giving them sudden piercing looks from different angles as if she could intimidate them into being asparagus.

"Wow," said Katherine. "A whole case."

"*Wow* is not the word I would have chosen. My goodness, it's not as if the boys require any *more* energy. That's all I need, children bouncing off the walls. Madeline, I don't mean you. Or Katherine. I know you two aren't"—Mrs. Vandermeer cleared her throat tactfully—"overly energetic."

This was a tiny sore point in Katherine's family. Mr. Vandermeer had been tremendously energetic in his youth and now worked a full-time job and coached five soccer teams. He was the epitome of oat bran–eating, jogging, weight-lifting health. Mrs. Vandermeer had been a cheerleader, a gymnast and a soccer player, and her scrapbooking was prodigious. She had masses of energy. The boys were all involved in sports every waking moment. They glowed with health and vigor. Katherine's favorite thing to do was to sit on the heating grate and stare into space.

When Katherine and Madeline did this in tandem, which

they did even when the heat wasn't on, Mrs. Vandermeer wondered what in the world was the matter with them, but she didn't have time to investigate. She was very, very busy. In the suburbs busyness was next to godliness. When Madeline, who loved the woods and ocean and all their entangled life-forms, saw the tiny treeless plots with the houses cheek by jowl—everything paved and cemented—she thought privately that people in the suburbs *needed* to be busy every second because if they stopped long enough to look around, they might notice where they were living.

"I wonder what these Pop-Tarts would do to *you*. . . ." Mrs. Vandermeer peered speculatively at the girls. For a second her maternal instincts were supplanted by scientific curiosity. Then she shook herself.

A car horn honked.

"Oh, the boys!" said Mrs. Vandermeer, looking at her watch. "We're going to be late for practice. Stop that honking!" she called, scurrying around to gather her things. "Katherine, be a dear and find some way to dispose of the Pop-Tarts before I get back with the boys. I don't want them to even *see* them."

Katherine nodded. It in no way interfered with her and Madeline's afternoon plan. They had the same plan pretty much every afternoon when Madeline came over. They went out to the gazebo, lay on the porch swing and the big wicker

recliner and read. Katherine and Madeline were each in the middle of a Louisa May Alcott book. Katherine was reading *Little Women* and Madeline was reading *Eight Cousins*. They never did chapter summaries at school. They simply refused. They never let anyone tell them *how* they should read a book or what they should think about it. They had too much respect for the books and the books' ability to speak for themselves.

"What to do with a case of Pop-Tarts? What to do with a case of Pop-Tarts?" said Katherine as they hoisted them out to the gazebo. She and Madeline flopped into their respective reading places and absentmindedly solved the problem by eating all but one box. That one Katherine shoved in Madeline's knapsack. Then they stomped on the carton and put it in recycling. By the time Mrs. Vandermeer got home, all traces of the Pop-Tarts were gone.

The girls were too sick for dinner that night and lay in Katherine's bunk beds moaning softly.

"I think we can state with scientific certainty that sugar does *not* give you excess energy," said Katherine as she lay greenly panting on the upper bunk. "I can't think of a time when I felt *less* like moving."

"Well, an entire case of sugar, anyway," said Madeline. "How's your book?"

"Fantastic. Laurie wants to marry Jo."

"Has Beth died yet?"

"WHAT?"

"Sorry."

They got out their flashlights—Mrs. Vandermeer made everyone turn off their lights at nine o'clock so they could start the next day fresh and energetic. Madeline and Katherine always dutifully turned off the light and then read by flashlight until midnight.

Now as Madeline packed her knapsack, she tossed the Pop-Tart box on the kitchen counter to make room for her nightgown and book. Then she ran to the porch, where Flo and Mildred were enjoying some rose hip tea and arguing about where they could travel on six dollars and twenty-seven cents.

"Oh well, Madeline will come up with something," said Flo. "Madeline always comes up with something."

Flo and Mildred depended on Madeline for quite a bit. She was their link with the real world. She seemed very adept at navigating it. They often said she was the real grown-up in the family.

If I could come up with a lot of money, thought Madeline, it would be going into my college education fund, not into a vacation that's here today and gone tomorrow. But she didn't say this. She gave them each a quick peck on the cheek and ran to catch the ferry.

And as it turned out, to everyone's surprise, it wasn't Madeline who came up with something. It was Flo.

# ⊧MRS. BUNNY HAS AN IDEA⊧

Mrs. Bunny, who was in bed recovering from a stirring bout of pneumonia, was signing a stack of copies of *Mr. and Mrs. Bunny—Detectives Extraordinaire!* It was her first book, and a rousing-good, almost-all-true account of the time she and Mr. Bunny had donned fedoras and helped Madeline find her parents, who had been kidnapped by foxes. The book had been wildly successful in the rabbit market and later translated into English, Marmot and even Fox, although in the fox market it was sold as a horror story. It had done so well that Mrs. Bunny decided to start writing a new one. She did not want to disappoint her fans. She began by making notes for the new book and stopped signing books whenever one of her brilliant observations came to her, such as now. She put down the book she was autographing and picked up the blank book where she kept her writing notes and scribbled:

> Mr. Bunny was not a good patient. He had a tendency to whine. Mrs. Bunny was an extraordinary patient with the temperament of a saint. She only wanted what was best for everyone in her path and made the sickroom a bower of peace and happiness.

Mr. Bunny, who was hanging out around Mrs. Bunny's sickbed dropping crumbs in her otherwise nice clean sheets, read what Mrs. Bunny had written and exploded with a snort.

It caused Mrs. Bunny to jump two feet in the air. This is not high for bunnies, but it is *very* high for *sick* bunnies who are lying down at the time, as Mrs. Bunny pointed out.

"Mr. Bunny, mercy, mercy, you gave me such a start! You should not make exploding noises around critically ill rabbits."

"Critically ill, my furry feet," said Mr. Bunny. "And when did you start saying things like *mercy, mercy?*"

"When I became a world-renowned author."

"Yes, and that is another sore point, Mrs. Bunny. You did not give me proper credit in that book at all."

"Whatever do you mean, Mr. Bunny? I did a lovely dedication to you."

"'To Mr. Bunny, of course!'" quoted Mr. Bunny bitterly. "What you should have said was '*By* Mr. Bunny, of course!' And right on the cover. All the best lines were mine. We could have written in very tiny print underneath, 'With some nominal help from Mrs. Bunny.' That would have been more accurate."

"Mr. Bunny, how you do run on. And if you wanted to be listed as a coauthor, why did you not say so before the book was published?"

"I was waiting for the reviews," said Mr. Bunny.

"No guts, no glory," said Mrs. Bunny, and settled comfortably back into her pillows.

"And another thing—in the next book, I think I should make up the chapter titles," said Mr. Bunny.

"You didn't like my chapter titles?" squealed Mrs. Bunny in dismay.

"I did not like *some* of them. For instance, the chapter titled 'Mrs. Bunny Worries That Prison Will Be Bad for Her Complexion.' That chapter should obviously have been called 'Mr. Bunny Gets a Summons to the Bunny Council But Isn't in the Least Distressed Because He Is a Very Brave Bunny.'"

"That's very wordy," said Mrs. Bunny, chewing on her pencil end. "And also not how I remember things at all."

"You've been ill," said Mr. Bunny. "Your memory is no doubt affected."

"Well, anyway, Bunny Publishing likes my chapter titles. I would not give them up."

"I am not suggesting you do," said Mr. Bunny. "I am suggesting that on the new book, we each make up a chapter title and readers will have to figure out which title is from whom."

"Oh, Mr. Bunny," said Mrs. Bunny, her ears quivering. "That is a very bold idea. It has never been done before."

"Exactly," said Mr. Bunny. "That's what you have me for. Bold ideas. Remember when I saved the day by having the bold idea to tell the Bunny Council that Madeline was our pet?"

"Yes, that's true . . . ," Mrs. Bunny said slowly. She had to admit, Mr. Bunny did have some remarkable ideas. And if they did not manifest in inventions of some kind, they often worked out. He was a smart rabbit; she would give him that. She would have to think about this. To stall she said, "Speaking of Madeline, why doesn't she visit? She does not even know I have been near death."

"No one knows you have been near death. It would certainly be news to the doctor," said Mr. Bunny under his breath.

"What's that?" snapped Mrs. Bunny, whose illness had not affected her long and fuzzy ears one iota.

"I was saying that Madeline will come when she can. You

know that. It is a very long way from Hornby Island, and she has many busy summer plans, no doubt."

"But it's been *AGES* and *AGES* since we saw her!" wailed Mrs. Bunny.

"It's been ten days. Get a grip," said Mr. Bunny.

"Yes, yes," said Mrs. Bunny, fidgeting with the bedcovers. "I suppose you are right."

"But still," said Mr. Bunny. "I see your point."

"She doesn't call," said Mrs. Bunny.

"She doesn't write," said Mr. Bunny.

They stared in a woebegone fashion at the wall for several minutes. Then Mrs. Bunny shook herself. "I must stop this. This is not like me. It is very like *you,* of course. But Mrs. Bunny is never of a martyry disposition. Madeline will come when she can. I'm sure if she knew I was recovering from a stirring bout of pneumonia, she would come in a trice. You *might* have written her and told her how worried you were, but we will let that go," said Mrs. Bunny. Then she realized she might use this grudge to her advantage in the future and added, "Maybe."

Mr. Bunny had indeed at one time been quite worried about Mrs. Bunny. It happened on a Tuesday and it lasted forty-seven seconds. Then the doctor told him that he was quite sure if she kept her fur warm and dry, she would recover rapidly. At which point Mr. Bunny switched to worrying about himself and who was going to make him carrot cakes in the interim. He did not like Mrs. Bunny getting sick. Worrying was a great inconvenience and so was ironing his own shirts. He made her many cups of carrot tea, but none of them managed to reach her without a good deal of grumbling attached.

"We are out of carrot cake," he said glumly.

Mrs. Bunny returned to scribbling feverishly in her writing notebook.

> Whatever Mr. Bunny was thinking had a tendency to come winging out of his mouth with no self-control.

Then, in a weak-and-cannot-bake-cakes voice, she replied, "There must be some still in the freezer."

"Prune cakes. A dozen of them. And that's another thing. What are we doing with a dozen prune cakes in our freezer? You know Mr. Bunny despises prune."

"Never mind that," said Mrs. Bunny hastily. "That is all explained in the last book. Which you would know if you *did,* as you *claim,* read the book all the way through."

"I may have skimmed the parts that didn't have Mr. Bunny in them . . . ," said Mr. Bunny reflectively.

"Well, I call that marmotlike," said Mrs. Bunny indignantly.

"Marmotlike? What about you taking all the credit for the writing of the bunny book *and* stocking the freezer with cakes Mr. Bunny does not like—"

"Never mind cake," interrupted Mrs. Bunny. "Let us move on. If you got your way what would you name *this* chapter? I would name it 'Mrs. Bunny Has an Idea' because—"

"Oh, I would probably name it 'Mr. Bunny Trembles in His Shoes Because Mrs. Bunny Is About to Try to Announce Some Perfectly Dreadful Thing That She Is Going to Force Mr. Bunny, Who Has No Desire Whatsoever to Do It, to Do with Her.'"

"You see, it is just as I feared. That's very wordy and full of repetition. And our chapter titles would contradict each other. It would only confuse readers in the end. I propose you drop the idea of naming them."

"I merely wish to defend my own bunny position on things. Sometimes I think you give the readers a very skewed vision of Mr. Bunny. Mr. Bunny should get to write the parts in which Mr. Bunny stars."

"Are there such parts?" Mrs. Bunny wondered aloud.

"There would be more if Mr. Bunny did the writing, you

can bet your fluffy tail on that. And you have to admit, it's only fair that Mr. Bunny should get to portray himself in an accurate fashion."

Mrs. Bunny chewed on her pencil. She could not find a way around this. "Oh, all right. I fear you will get it all wrong as usual, Mr. Bunny, but there is no sense trying to talk you out of it. It will have to be between you and the editor. Now let us move on, because none of that is really here or there. I have an important announcement. As I lie here breathing my last, Mr. Bunny, I am having thoughts."

"That would be a first, Mrs. Bunny," said Mr. Bunny. "A first during your last."

"Ha ha. You are a humorous rabbit. Not. As I say, as I lie here on my bed of pain—"

"Bed of *pain*? Have I not bought you six new white and fluffy pillows?" interrupted Mr. Bunny. "Just as you requested."

"Yes, but you bought them on sale. At Bunny-Mart. They are already squished, Mr. Bunny. If you were lying at death's door, I would be toodling to Bunnydale's to get you the very best in downy goodness."

"No doubt," said Mr. Bunny. "But it takes very little to encourage you to toodle, as you call it, to Bunnydale's."

Bunnydale's was the new high-end department store that

had opened in Rabbitville. Mrs. Bunny and all her fellow hat clubbers had been busily putting themselves in debt since it opened.

"Whatever," said Mrs. Bunny. "Let's hear no more about my pillows."

"I merely wish to point out that you can't be in pain on new pillows. It's unseemly," said Mr. Bunny. "Indeed, I think it's a physical impossibility."

"I may be in pain because you will not let me finish a thought. As I say, as I lie here beleaguered, aching but sweet and cheerful as usual, I cast back upon my life and the many dreams I had as a girl. Why, I ask myself, why, Mrs. Bunny, have you not done these things you always meant to do?"

"Uh-oh," said Mr. Bunny. "Now we're in for it."

"Mr. Bunny, bunnies who are ill need nurturing and many, many compliments. Otherwise they sink into a decline and can never more bake carrot cakes for their bunny pals."

This shut Mr. Bunny up.

Mrs. Bunny smiled bravely and continued. "What has been occupying my bunny brains is that when I am well enough to hop about again, we will want a brand-new profession."

"I thought you had already chosen one. I thought we were to be authors."

"Writers, Mr. Bunny, need something to write *about*," said

Mrs. Bunny. "What I had in mind was a series of books in which I could write about our new professions. A book for each profession. *My Life as a Bunny-Mart Greeter. My Life as a Neuroscientist. My Life as the Easter Bunny.*"

"There is only one Easter Bunny," Mr. Bunny pointed out.

"Yes, but he cannot live forever," said Mrs. Bunny placidly. "And with each new profession we need new hats."

"Ah," said Mr. Bunny.

At the end of Mr. and Mrs. Bunny's last adventure, in which they had been detectives, they had tossed out their fedoras. Mrs. Bunny was not sure Mr. Bunny remembered this. He was a little vague when it came to hats.

"Remember the gay abandon with which we tossed out our fedoras? In case, we said at the time, we were tempted to don them and do same old, same old. Nobody likes a repeater bunny. We did not wish to get stuck in any *RUTS,* Mr. Bunny."

"We wanted to buy a new hat is how I read it," Mr. Bunny said.

"Perhaps. But as you will recall, Mr. Bunny," said Mrs. Bunny, further pulling herself into a sitting position against the pillows, the better to become emphatic, "we never did shop for new hats. I fell into a decline too quickly. But now, as my strength returns, my mind casts about for some profession for us. Let us bat about a few ideas."

"Unless I am a much less clever bunny than I think, my guess is you have already picked a profession for us and by 'bat about a few ideas' mean you are now ready to bully Mr. Bunny into adopting it."

"Bingo!" said Mrs. Bunny.

# ⊁FLO FINDS HIS CALLING⊀

Flo and Mildred were preparing to head over to Zanky's.

"Grab a bottle of my homemade dandelion wine," said Mildred as she gathered her things.

Flo went to the cupboard. "All gone," he said sadly.

"Gone? I told you I was saving a bottle to bring to dinner."

"I forgot. Anyhow, it doesn't matter. Zanky makes her own dandelion wine."

"Not the point. We have to bring something. It's only polite. How about some of my carob truffles?"

This time Flo didn't even need to go to the cupboard. "Gone."

"My organic carrot leather?"

"Uh. Gone."

"Well, this is a pretty pickle. We can't go over with NOTHING."

"Uh, how about this?" asked Flo in desperation, grabbing a turnip from the fridge.

"You can't bring a turnip as a hostess present. Honestly, Flo, you knew as well as I did we were going for dinner tonight. You might have . . ."

Flo tried to shut his ears as Mildred droned on when suddenly his eyes fell on the box of Pop-Tarts Madeline had left on the counter.

"Hey, what about *these*?" he said.

"Where did those come from?" asked Mildred.

"A merciful universe," Flo muttered to himself.

Mildred picked up the box and read the label. "There's nothing organic in here at all."

"Never mind," said Flo, taking the box from her. "Zanky will be too busy with her guests to notice."

Flo was right. Zanky had twenty-seven dear friends for dinner, and everyone was so busy greeting everyone else that the Pop-Tarts were just tossed onto the kitchen counter, their ingredients unread. But as the evening went on and candles were lit and various Zen practices discussed, folk songs sung and chants chanted, with people settling into a state of happy spirituality, the food began to run out.

"Hey, what's this?" asked Meadowbrook.

"Pop-Tarts," said Flo, who was standing next to Meadowbrook as she examined the box.

"Can you eat them?" she asked.

Flo looked at the box again. "I think," he said uncertainly.

"There's only six," said Meadowbrook, ripping open the package. "And I'm starving."

"No one says we have to share," said Flo. They sneaked out to the gazebo and tried to stuff them in before anyone else came along.

"WOW!" said Meadowbrook. "These are the best things I've ever eaten."

"I know," said Flo. "What's in them that's so tasty?" He picked up the box and read the label. "Sugar," he said in surprise. "That's the main ingredient. I haven't had any for years. I'd almost forgotten about the stuff. Was it always this good? I think they improved it. I want more."

"Me too," said Meadowbrook. "Maybe we could, like, swim to the mainland and get some?"

"No, man, there's sharks out there. Let's just chill."

They rocked back and forth in the gazebo swing until it

made them too dizzy. "So, are you, like, visiting the island?" asked Flo.

"Yeah, we can only stay for two days. We're at the campground and it costs sixty bucks a night for a little ten-by-ten site."

"Wow," said Flo.

"Yeah," said Meadowbrook. "Quite a racket."

"Wow," said Flo.

"I mean ripping off the tourists that way. I think camping should be, like, free."

"Oh, like, totally," said Flo.

"We couldn't have even afforded the campground, but Sunset and I got a gig with our marimba band last winter on a cruise ship. We got free passage and sometimes we would busk in ports and pick up some money on the side."

"Cool."

"Yeah. We just got called to do another gig, but I get seasick. Hey, we missed one," said Meadowbrook, pulling the last Pop-Tart out of the box. "Split it?"

"Thanks," said Flo, taking a big bite out of his half. "Oh MAN, that's good. I mean, it beats the pants off carob truffles. Don't tell Mildred I said that. Oh MAN. I'm, like, having a revelation here. Sugar is, like, a *good* thing. Do people know this? I don't think they do. You know, I feel a calling. I gotta bring this to the people. The people are where it's at. The people and . . . sugar."

"Gee," said Meadowbrook, looking at him in awe. "I'm witnessing a big moment here."

"Yeah. You bet. For the rest of my life, I'm, like, devoting myself to sugar. I'm gonna be the Dalai Lama of sugar."

"Gee . . . ," said Meadowbrook. "The Dalai Lama of sugar."

Mildred came across the garden and joined them. They rocked some more and watched an owl chasing chipmunks.

"Man, I bet that owl doesn't know how much better those chipmunks would be sugarcoated," said Flo.

"I think it's time to go," said Mildred.

On the way home Flo told Mildred he was planning to devote the rest of his life to sugar.

"In what capacity?" asked Mildred.

"I don't know, man. I just know that this is my path."

"Huh," said Mildred. "Interesting. Flo, I want to buy that thirty acres going for sale next to us. Zanky owns it and she doesn't want to farm it. She said she'd sell it to me for thirty thousand dollars."

"Cool," said Flo. "But isn't that, like, really cheap?"

"Yeah, but Zanky doesn't want to sell it to anyone who will build on it or use it for anything but organic gardening, so she's willing to sacrifice. Zanky doesn't care about money.

And listen, you know Zanky has ten acres of her own under cultivation. She's doing really well selling her vegetables at the Comox farmers' market. Everyone is looking to buy locally. It's a whole movement. Even people in the suburbs and city want organically, locally grown food. We could really make a difference. We could bring wholesome healthy chemical-free food to the people."

"Go for it."

"I can't go for it. We don't have thirty thousand dollars. We don't have any money at all."

"We have six dollars and twenty-seven cents," said Flo sleepily as they floated up their driftwood-lined walkway in the light fragrant evening summer air. Flo collapsed on the couch on their porch and continued, "The Dalai Lama of sugar and the Mother Teresa of vegetables. It must be meant to be because it's, like, all the food groups."

Then he fell into a deep snoring slumber while Mildred watched the constellations twinkling through the porch screen and wondered if anything would come of their dreams, or if it would be like the time they decided to make a pedestrian walkway across Canada out of bottle caps.

The next day as Mildred and Flo walked to town to get their mail, Mildred was surprised to find that Flo was every bit as enthusiastic about his sugar plans as he had been the night before.

"But I still don't get *how* you are going to be the Dalai Lama of sugar," said Mildred plaintively after he had asserted this nineteen times.

"Mildred, I'm telling you. I've got a feeling about this. Like the universe is coalescing. Synchronicity. Everything is synchronicity. I can feel it. Can't you?"

"I can feel something."

"SEE?" said Flo, waving his arms around excitedly.

"But I think it's a pebble in my shoe. I need new shoes." Mildred sighed. "I wish we had more than six dollars."

"Don't forget the twenty-seven cents," said Flo cheerfully.

They reached the post office and went in. Mildred sorted through the week's worth of flyers and junk mail before pulling out a thick cream envelope.

"What's this?" she said. "It's for you, Flo."

"You read it; I'm meditating on the *cube*," said Flo. "*Sugar* cubes!"

"Right," said Mildred, examining the postmark. "England? Do you know anyone in England?"

"Nope," said Flo.

She ripped it open and read the letter inside twice. "Flo, do you have an Aunt Beatrice and an Uncle Bert?"

"Yeah, I've never met them but I send them my solstice letter every year. Someday, like, they should come to our winter solstice fete."

"Too late. They're dead. A car accident."

"Oh man, that's too bad. Being dead must really suck."

"It says they owned a sweet shoppe. And, Flo, listen to *this*, they left it to us."

"To us? Why us?"

*"Because,"* Mildred read, *"Flo and Mildred are the only relatives flaky enough to drop everything and go to England and run our beloved sweet shoppe.* Honestly, Flo, I don't know if that was supposed to be a *compliment.* Anyhow, the lawyer goes on to say that if we *don't* go there and keep their beloved sweet shoppe running, then it gets sold and the money goes to The Society for Depraved Cats."

"I don't know, Mildred, I don't like taking money away from the cats."

"FLO! Pay attention and *think.* If we go, we *own* a candy store. And the apartment over it. In *England.*"

*"A candy store."*

"Yes."

*"Sugar."*

"Yes."

*"Someplace to go."*

"Yes."

"Synchronicity," said Flo.

"This lawyer says the sweet shoppe has been 'a profitable fixture' in the village of Bellyflop for some time."

"Cool."

"Yes, very cool, Flo, because that must mean that it *makes money*. If we take on the running of it, then we will *make money*. What does the lawyer say here? Last year in the month of August alone it made one hundred thousand pounds. Flo, if we take over and run the shoppe this August we'll have more than enough money to buy Zanky's thirty acres!"

"Then we could, like, give the rest to the cats? 'Cause I really feel bad about those cats, man. I mean, what has to happen to a cat that it becomes *depraved*?"

"Yes, Flo, whatever. The only problem," said Mildred, biting on her knuckle, "is we have to find a way to *get* there."

# MRS. BUNNY'S
## LONG-STANDING DREAM

It was several evenings after Mrs. Bunny's great recovery that she finally spilled the beans about her plans for herself and Mr. Bunny. Mr. Bunny had said many times that he was all ears, but Mrs. Bunny said she was awaiting the perfect stellar moment. It came one lovely summer's eve with butterflies flitting about the hollyhocks, a freshly baked carrot cake (Mrs. Bunny was no novice when it came to springing plans on Mr. Bunny), some just-squeezed beet juice and the pleasant burble of the water feature Mrs. Bunny had installed in the flower garden, a recent addition, which drove Mr. Bunny nuts because you could not turn it off.

"Don't you find it soothing?" Mrs. Bunny asked Mr. Bunny

while placidly knitting next year's long underwear out of used dental floss.

"Mrs. Bunny, I do not ALWAYS wish to be soothed. Sometimes I like to be WORKED UP!"

"Nonsense," said Mrs. Bunny. "Think of your blood pressure."

"I can think of little else since you put that water fountain in."

"Water *feature*. Have some cake," said Mrs. Bunny, cutting him a large piece.

"Mumble, mumble," said Mr. Bunny. It was very difficult to remonstrate with a mouth full of nuts and raisins. Mrs. Bunny smiled smugly.

"Now, Mr. Bunny, we've had two weeks since our last adventure ended. It is time we delved into something else."

"Mumble, mumble," said Mr. Bunny.

"I knew you would agree. And as I lay upon my bed of pain, looking back on my life and my girlhood dreams, I realized there was one ambition that I had yet to fulfill."

"Mumble, mumble," said Mr. Bunny. Then he swallowed. "You're not going to start going on again about 'teaching the world to sing in perfect harmony,' are you?"

"Mr. Bunny, that was a Coke commercial."

"You seemed very adamant at the time."

"It was just a catchy tune. No, this is serious," said Mrs. Bunny, cutting him another piece of cake. "And I would like you to be serious for a change."

"Mumble, mumble," said Mr. Bunny. Then he swallowed. "You're not going to suggest as you once did that someone should 'fly you to the moon and let you play among the stars'?"

"That was after a Frank Sinatra special. Really, Mr. Bunny, anyone would think you could not tell the difference between Mrs. Bunny's career ambitions and her musical renditions. Have some more cake." She cut Mr. Bunny another thin slice.

"I give up," said Mr. Bunny, taking another big bite.

"I want to be queen!" squealed Mrs. Bunny.

Mr. Bunny swallowed. "I hope you are kidding."

"Why would I kid about such a thing?" asked Mrs. Bunny somewhat testily. She had sat up very tall when she had made her announcement and had anticipated a response more along the lines of "and how a tiara would *suit* you, Mrs. Bunny!" "I've been thinking of it ever since I saw Prince Charles give out the awards at Madeline's school. How well he deported himself. What a charming man. *I'm* a charming bunny. *I* should be royal."

"Look, Mrs. Bunny, I have indulged your various ventures in the past, worn fedoras, chased about after secret decoders, but I will be darned if I'm going to put on a crown."

"Who said anything about you? Indeed, I had envisioned you more as a footman," said Mrs. Bunny reflectively.

"A . . . ," Mr. Bunny began, then calmed down and reminded himself that Mrs. Bunny had recently had a fever. No doubt her brains had fried. "Have some more beet juice," he said kindly, and poured her a glass.

"You see, you'd make an excellent footman," said Mrs. Bunny.

"I am not going to be a footman," said Mr. Bunny. "Whatever else may happen, I can promise you that."

"Well, then you could be like Prince Philip. Nobody really knows what he is."

"What are you talking about? He's a prince. It says so right in his name."

"How can he be? His son Prince Charles is a prince. How can they both be princes?"

"I do not know. The vagaries of the monarchy are beyond me," said Mr. Bunny, cutting himself yet more cake. He suspected quite rightly that Mrs. Bunny was not going to comment on his cake consumption while petitioning him to aid in making her queen. "Anyhow, Mrs. Bunny, you cannot be queen. There is already a queen. And you have to be born into the monarchy. You cannot simply decide one day that that's it, it's queen time or something."

"I'm not so sure about that, Mr. Bunny. Don't you remember when Sarah Ferguson married Prince Andrew and they just made her a duchess on the spot? That's what they do, they just pick titles out of the air and give them to people. 'Here, you be a duchess,' they say, 'and you over there, guess what, yesterday you were nothing, today you're an earl.' Why, it's *nothing* for Queen Elizabeth to make me a queen. She's got all those titles at her disposal just lying around waiting for a deserving bunny. And besides, the queen is a *human* queen. Isn't it time there was a queen of the bunnies?"

"Well, time or not, it looks like a thankless job to me," said Mr. Bunny.

"No, no, it isn't at all!" squealed Mrs. Bunny, losing her studied cool. "You get to live in a castle and wear pretty dresses and go to balls!"

"I am almost certain there is more to it than that," said Mr. Bunny. "Besides, you said that this was our next adventure. What's in it for me?"

"The knowledge that you have helped Mrs. Bunny fulfill a long-standing dream. Also, probably, a carrot cake a day for life."

"Hmmm," said Mr. Bunny.

"What's this about daily cakes?" came a familiar voice, and Mrs. Treaclebunny hopped into the yard. Mrs. Treaclebunny

lived across the way. She often came over to borrow the Bunnys' lawn fertilizers and carrot scrapers and dental picks,
toothpaste and toilet-bowl cleaner. She just as often came over
uninvited for dinner. The Bunnys had never been able to figure
out what to do about her. Now she settled herself happily into
one of the Bunnys' lawn chairs and grabbed a piece of cake.

"Yum," she said.

"Have some cake," said Mr. Bunny dryly.

"Don't mind if I do," she said, jamming the last bite into
her cheek and cutting a second slice. "You know, if you added
some grated zucchini to this, it wouldn't be so dry and taste-
less."

Mr. Bunny tore at his ears, but Mrs. Treaclebunny never
seemed to notice such things.

"I was just telling Mr. Bunny that I would like to be queen,"
said Mrs. Bunny. "It's a long-standing dream of mine."

"I see," said Mrs. Treaclebunny. "Well, it wouldn't suit *me*.
Have to go around cutting ribbons and shaking paws. No,
thank you. I suspect you're off to England, then."

"England?" said Mrs. Bunny.

"Oh yes, you can't become queen here. If you want to become queen you have to go to England and get coronated."

"What, may I ask, is *coronated*?" asked Mr. Bunny. "It
sounds painful."

"Oh, it is. That's when they clap a crown on your ears."

"A very heavy crown, I should imagine," said Mr. Bunny. "No doubt your ears never fluff properly again."

"It's a big deal," Mrs. Treaclebunny went on. "Lots of other royalty show up. They're all in each other's pockets: the German royalty, the French royalty, the Iowan royalty."

"Oh, Mr. Bunny!" said Mrs. Bunny. "We would have duchessy pals!"

"Oh yeah," said Mrs. Treaclebunny. "And I suspect Hollywood sends a few stars and there's a red carpet and people taking your picture and you get in all the magazines."

"You certainly seem to know a lot about it," said Mr. Bunny stiffly.

"Oh yes, Mr. Treaclebunny—God rest his poor dead desiccated paws—and I used to follow it all. We were quite the royalty buffs. *Hello!* magazine stays on those royalty like white on rice. Anyhow, I know that when it happens, it happens in England, so if you really want to be queen, Mrs. Bunny, you'd better just skedaddle yourself across the pond."

"What pond?" asked Mr. Bunny.

"Bunnies who are really sophisticated call the *Atlantic Ocean* the pond," said Mrs. Treaclebunny in her most superior tone. Her property across the way had an *ocean view*. It had always been a sore point with Mr. and Mrs. Bunny.

"Oh, Mr. Bunny, a trip! We haven't taken a trip since . . . ever. And we could go by ship and Mrs. Bunny could pack all her long sparkly formal gowns and we could dance cheek to cheek to the ship's orchestra every night and gaze at the moonlight on the open waters of the great sea!"

"How very poetic, Mrs. Bunny. We must get you your own spot on National Public Radio," said Mr. Bunny. "But what formal gowns are you talking about? I know I have only a passing acquaintance with your wardrobe, but I do not recall ever seeing any long sparkly formal gowns."

"Well, of course I shall have to *shop* for those," said Mrs. Bunny.

"At Bunnydale's," said Mrs. Treaclebunny, and she and Mrs. Bunny nodded to each other.

Bunnydale's had the first long sparkly formal gown department in Rabbitville, and all the female bunnies had been plotting occasions to wear them. So far this had been a bust. All of Mrs. Bunny's female friends except for Mrs. Treaclebunny were in a hat club with her. It was their unhappy conclusion, after much discussion, that Rabbitville was an unfortunately casual sort of town.

"I see," said Mr. Bunny. "Mrs. Bunny, you know my one tried-and-true credo is never leave the hutch! It's inevitably expensive and tedious and dangerous. Travel is—"

"Yes, I know," said Mrs. Bunny hastily. "Tedium relieved by terror. But, Mr. Bunny, how can I be coronated if we don't leave the hutch?"

"You can't," said Mrs. Treaclebunny, helping herself to the rest of the carrot cake.

"For years I have been carting home brochures for foreign climes only to have something come up. Usually a baby bunny," said Mrs. Bunny confidentially to Mrs. Treaclebunny. Mr. and Mrs. Bunny had twelve children but they were all grown and gone.

"Well," said Mr. Bunny, clearly wavering, "you're not getting me on an airplane."

"They make you go in a *crate,*" said Mrs. Bunny to Mrs. Treaclebunny. "In *storage.* And they don't even give you any drinks or peanuts."

"And then they quarantine you for two weeks," said Mrs. Treaclebunny. "You needn't tell *me.* Mr. Treaclebunny once traveled to England on business that way and he never fully recovered. After that, when we made our European jaunts it was ocean liners for us!"

"Exactly. An ocean voyage with long sparkly formal gowns is certainly the way to go. No pooey airplanes, you are *so* right, Mr. Bunny. You *are* a discerning rabbit. Carrot cakes for life, carrot cakes for life," chanted Mrs. Bunny in what she hoped was a hypnotic fashion. "Besides, you promised. Even though you hate leaving the hutch, you said that someday after the baby bunnies were grown you would take a trip with me."

"Curses," said Mr. Bunny resignedly. "Hoisted with my own rabbito petard. But I am nothing if not fair. Humph! Well, you'd better keep those carrot cakes coming, that's all I can say. In the meantime, I'll get the suitcases out of the basement."

"Excellent," said Mrs. Treaclebunny, sitting back and pouring herself a fourth cup of beet juice. "When do we leave?"

## BON VOYAGE

When Madeline got home from her weekend at Katherine's she found Flo and Mildred standing on the porch. Next to them were three suitcases.

"What are you *wearing*?" asked Madeline in shock.

Flo had on a brightly printed Hawaiian shirt over a pair of flowing white pants. Mildred was wearing aqua pedal pushers with a beaded tunic. They both had on straw hats and new sandals.

"Gee, I would have thought she would ask about the suitcases first," said Flo.

"Or the people all over our property," said Mildred.

"I was going to ask about that, but . . ." Madeline took a step closer and fingered Mildred's shiny tunic. "Is that *polyester*?"

"I don't know, I haven't had time to look at the label," said Mildred, handing Madeline a neat pile of similar clothes. "We've had a lot to do in a short time. We just came back from shopping for cruisewear this afternoon. Here's yours. Everything's new. Even your sandals are new."

"We've been *very busy,*" said Flo.

"I can see that," said Madeline. "But busy doing what? Who are all those people in tents on our land? What are these suitcases for? Where did you get these clothes? Didn't you once say that you'd rather be eaten by squirrels than wear man-made fibers?"

"Well, Flo has been having ideas," said Mildred. "I know you have a lot of questions, but you'll have to ask them later. Stan is giving us a ride and we have to leave right now if we're going to get to Victoria in time to make our cruise ship."

"Where are we going?" asked Madeline.

"To England," said Flo. "We're becoming confectioners."

Madeline rubbed her eyes as if she could bring reality back in focus this way, but when she stopped a man was coming over and putting the suitcases into the trunk of his car.

"Who's *that?*" asked Madeline.

"Don't be rude," said Mildred. "That's Stan. He's getting a discount on his campsite by driving us to Victoria.

You see, your father was talking to Meadowbrook Saturday night. . . ."

"I'm sorry, who?"

"Never mind, it's not important. Get in the car," said Mildred, hustling Madeline into the backseat. Stan pulled away and they sped toward the ferry terminal. "You remember we said we'd be at Zanky's for dinner? Well, this Meadowbrook was there and she told Flo that she was paying sixty dollars a night for a ten-by-ten-foot spot in the campground, so Flo had this great idea. . . ."

"Don't know why I never thought of it before," said Flo.

"To undersell the campground and rent out our property to campers for *fifty* bucks for a ten-by-ten space. We sold out all our spaces immediately. Of course, it means people will be sleeping on our carrots, but that's all right because we won't be around to harvest them anyway."

"So then who is going to run the campground?"

"Zanky. For half the profits. We already made a couple thousand dollars!" said Flo.

"Enough to buy cruisewear. We've been shopping all afternoon and making phone calls. It's been a whirlwind."

"So we're using it to take a cruise?" asked Madeline.

"Actually, we're going to England for the summer because

Aunt Beatrice and Uncle Bert were killed in a car accident. They owned a candy store."

"I've always wanted to run a candy store," said Stan from the driver's seat.

"Who are Beatrice and Bert?" asked Madeline, ignoring Stan.

"They're a couple of dead relatives. They wanted us to have the candy store," said Mildred.

"Well, either us or the cats," said Flo.

"What cats?" asked Madeline.

"Forget about the cats," said Mildred. "Anyhow, according to the lawyer, the sweet shoppe is a gold mine, so we're going to make enough to buy Zanky's thirty acres and then we can bring wholesome organic food to the people."

"And sugar," said Flo. "I'm the Dalai Lama of sugar and your mother is going to be the Mother Teresa of vegetables."

Madeline shook her head. This was the biggest project her parents had started since they decided to pave Canada in bottle caps. "And we have to leave *right now*?"

"Yes, because our marimba band got a gig on a ship that is leaving Victoria tonight," said Flo. "Meadowbrook's marimba band originally got offered the gig but they didn't want it, and so I called the cruise ship, asked if they were still looking for a marimba band and said we would do it. We don't get paid, but we get free passage for our family. So we gotta hustle. Cool, huh? I've had so many ideas this weekend, my brain is, like, smoking."

"That's great. That's great," murmured Madeline as her mind frantically went over the details. "But are you sure this whole thing isn't something you, uh, imagined Saturday night?"

Mildred passed Madeline the lawyer's letter. Madeline read it twice.

"I guess it's true," she said finally.

"It's synchronicity," said Flo. "And it all started when a box of Pop-Tarts materialized on our countertop. It was, like, mystical and magical, man. It was the universe pointing the way."

"Pop-Tarts? They didn't magically and mystically appear, Katherine put them in my . . . Oh my gosh, Katherine was supposed to be coming to the island tomorrow. I invited her to spend the week and now we won't be there!"

"Do you want to call your friend?" asked Stan, and passed her his cell phone.


At home Katherine was pacing around. Six of her brother Ned's friends were bouncing a basketball in the driveway. Four of William's friends were playing street hockey out front. Eight of Robert's friends were hitting a baseball in the backyard. And three of Kevin's friends were running around the house at full speed, screaming, "MARCO POLO!" She could hardly hear the phone ring.

"Hello," she said, picking it up on its eighth ring. "Madeline, is that you? You'll have to shout."

"Katherine, you're not going to believe this. I'm getting on the ferry. We're driving down to Victoria and taking a ship to England."

A basketball came flying through the window and hit Katherine in the head.

"MOM!" she screamed to Mrs. Vandermeer, who was scrapbooking at the kitchen table. "I can't even hear Madeline. Why do all the boys have to be here and why do they all have to play ball and run around and scream?"

"I know it's noisy," said Mrs. Vandermeer. "But do what I'm about to do and put in some earplugs."

"Why can't they do something quiet like read?"

"Because if they don't have a constructive energetic sporting outlet, they will become juvenile delinquents, and from there it's a short hop to prison, where there's a high rate of recidivism. Then they'll be career criminals. Is that what you want for your brothers?" Without waiting for an answer, Mrs. Vandermeer put in a pair of earplugs and went back to scrapbooking.

Katherine put the phone back to her ear. "Take me with you."

"Wouldn't that be great?" asked Madeline, sighing.

"I'm serious. I don't care if you're going to a swamp or Death Valley. Just get me out of here. I'm going insane. I can't stand it. OUCH! I keep getting hit with stray balls. I'm bruised all over. You know what it is? It's recreational abuse!"

"But we're leaving right now."

"I'm a fast packer."

"Just a minute," said Madeline.

Katherine heard Madeline asking someone something and then Flo came on the phone.

"Madeline says you want to go to England with us. That's cool. We'll have Stan get you on our way down to Victoria. But there's just one thing. You gotta, like, pretend to be part of our family, okay? You gotta look the part."

"Why?" asked Katherine.

But the phone went into a dead zone and the explanation was lost.

Katherine ran to the kitchen and ripped out one of her mother's earplugs.

"Can I leave right now for England?" she shouted to her mother.

"Please do," said Mrs. Vandermeer. "And take me with you."

Katherine ran upstairs to pack. She threw her most ragged summer clothes and a collection of summer reading into her suitcase. Then she carefully dressed to look like part of Madeline's family in a skirt that was a little too big, her most scuffed-up shoes and an old peasant blouse. She ran downstairs and outside to await Madeline's car.

"Where are you going?" asked Mrs. Vandermeer, coming out to the porch and eyeing the suitcase and Katherine's peculiar outfit.

"I'm going to England. You said I could. Gotta run. My ride's here!"

Stan pulled into the driveway, just as one of the hockey players was hit by a passing bike. The bike rider and the hockey player lay in a tumble of equipment, screaming at the top of their lungs. Mrs. Vandermeer ran over to disentangle the boys from the bikes from the hockey sticks.

When she looked up, Flo was putting Katherine's suitcase in the trunk.

"We gotta run! Ship's waiting. See you in September! Don't worry about a thing, the synchronicity has kicked in. The universe is, like, caring for us, man!" called Flo, getting back into the car.

"The what?" Katherine asked Madeline.

"I'll explain on the drive down," said Madeline, who had already been apprised of Flo's new theory.

Then five sets of hands waved jauntily from the windows as the car sped down the road.

"Wait a second, I thought you were kidding!" called Mrs. Vandermeer to the fleeing car.

But it was too late. The car turned the corner and then they were gone.

# ◄SHIPBOARD BUNNIES►

"**I**t was very nice of the hat club to send a fruit basket to our stateroom," said Mrs. Bunny with a note of false cheer. She was putting on her long sparkly formal gown for their first shipboard dinner.

"Nothing about this cruise bears any resemblance to the brochures," grumbled Mr. Bunny, struggling into his tuxedo shirt. His furry tummy kept bursting through between the buttons. That was what it was to be a rabbit. Endless tucking in of loose fur. "Those big staterooms in the pictures?" Mr. Bunny looked around the tiny room he and Mrs. Bunny were sharing. There were two tiny twin beds and practically nowhere for their luggage. "Not."

"Oh dear," said Mrs. Bunny as she tried on her earrings. It was difficult to wear dangling earrings when your ears were so long. Her earrings kept dangling down into her ear canals. "Too much?" She was hoping to distract Mr. Bunny from his mood of doom and gloom. So far nothing about this trip was as she had promised. It wasn't "Better than home!" "Full of luxury and expensive free bath products for Mrs. Bunny!" "Endless service at no extra cost!" "Huge stateroom with quality linens!" So far it was just a small room in the sub-sub-basement level of the ship. That they would not be riding up on top, she already knew. The bunny cruises did at least tell you the animal deck was below the human one. Unfortunately, although the brochures stated this plainly, the pictures they provided were for the human quarters. It was very trying to be a vacationing rabbit.

"Well, there had better just be a gym. Mr. Bunny needs his hopping," said Mr. Bunny.

Mrs. Bunny sighed again.

At that moment there was a knock on the door. Mr. Bunny was trying to get his bow tie to lie evenly over a particularly cumbersome tuft of fur, so Mrs. Bunny answered it.

It was Mrs. Treaclebunny. "Do you have any Flit?" she asked. "I forgot to pack mine. Always take it when traveling to spray the beds. You never know. Bugs. For all we know, Bug Cruises are putting their travelers up in our rooms. Saves a lot of money for them."

"I'm sure there are no bugs on this ship," said Mrs. Bunny.

"Well, perhaps not in *my* room," said Mrs. Treaclebunny, looking critically around Mr. and Mrs. Bunny's cramped quarters. She settled herself on Mrs. Bunny's bed. "You must have gone for the economy package."

"We did," said Mr. Bunny. "I'm not shelling out twice the fare for a slightly bigger room."

"Slightly? You could fit ten of your rooms in my room. . . ." Mrs. Treaclebunny's voice trailed off as she looked around. "And where's your champagne and chompies?"

"Chompies?" asked Mrs. Bunny.

"You know, little bite-sized edibles. They always bring them to you before dinner and before bed. That's what Mr. Treaclebunny and I called them. So many and so varied and so rich. We could never finish them although we chomped for all we were worth."

"We, uh, didn't get any chompies," said Mrs. Bunny, looking close to tears.

"Not included in the economy package," said Mr. Bunny. "Who needs them. Look what Mr. Bunny brought!" He went over to his suitcase and triumphantly pulled out a large jar of Cheez Whiz and a box of saltines. "We can make our own chompies!" He proceeded to spread Cheez Whiz on a cracker, getting Cheez Whiz and cracker crumbs everywhere in the attempt. "There," he said when he had managed a few that didn't simply disintegrate all over the floor. He removed some soap packets from a little plastic tray in the bathroom, put his homemade chompies on it and served them forth. "Anyone for a chompie?"

Mrs. Bunny and Mrs. Treaclebunny quickly declined. Mrs. Bunny looked closer to tears than ever.

"Anyhow," said Mrs. Treaclebunny, getting up and spinning around, "what do you think of the dress?"

Both Mrs. Bunny and Mrs. Treaclebunny had been frequenting Bunnydale's with some regularity for the last couple of days. It was one reason the Bunnys were going economy class.

"It's ravishing," said Mrs. Bunny truthfully. Mrs. Treaclebunny was a vision in red sequins. Mrs. Bunny was starting slow with her black chiffon. She wanted to see how sparkly the other bunnies dressed before pulling out the big guns.

"Are you sitting first or second dinner service?" asked Mrs. Treaclebunny. "Second service is the smart one."

"We're sitting first service," said Mr. Bunny. "It's part of our economy package. I much prefer it myself. I do not like having to wait much past five o'clock for my dinner."

"Well, looks like I won't be seeing much of you, then," said Mrs. Treaclebunny, getting up and laughing. "I'm at second service myself. Toodle-oo." And she waltzed out the door.

"Come on, Mrs. Bunny," said Mr. Bunny, jovially taking her elbow and leading her out of their stateroom. "Don't want to be last at the trough."

"Oh my goodness," said Mrs. Bunny when they entered the dining room. "Did you think it would be like this? I guess I imagined . . ."

The dining room was a cacophony of noise. There was a large buffet and racing around it, packed in like sardines, were pigs, goats, marmots, cats and dogs. Birds flew about overhead, dipping their beaks into the steam-table vats and removing choice morsels.

"I guess, I guess it didn't occur to me that other species took cruises," whispered Mrs. Bunny.

"Not all on cruises," said the waiter at her elbow. "At first service we also take care of all the pets traveling in crates in the hold. They are allowed to get out, stretch their legs, have a dip at the buffet. Poor things."

"But you don't have any . . . f . . . f . . . f . . . ?" said Mrs. Bunny, grabbing Mr. Bunny's arm for support as the thought occurred to her.

"Foxes?" whispered the waiter. "No, ma'am. Even economy class has its standards. Now what I recommend is you belly up to that buffet before it's all gone."

"I thought . . ." Mrs. Bunny's voice trailed off as a particularly large pig ambled by, carrying a bucket of food to her table. " . . . that dinner would be rather refined. That there were endless courses and a large menu and gourmet food . . . the picture in the brochure."

"Not at first service, ma'am," said the waiter sympathetically. "And not in economy. And in second service it's"—his voice dropped to a whisper—"mostly just bunnies. And if you don't mind me saying so, a better *class* of bunnies." Then his voice went back to normal. "As for the menu in second service . . . whoops, gotta go. The birds have just pooped in the Swedish meatballs again. I'd steer clear of those, if I were you."

"Well . . . ," said Mr. Bunny. "Uh, shall we?"

"I don't think I'm hungry anymore," whispered Mrs. Bunny.

"Me either," said Mr. Bunny, and they went sadly back to their stateroom and ate a few dry crackers.

The Bunnys read their books for a while, and then the ship began furiously rocking.

"Mr. Bunny, I think I would feel better if I could stroll about. My tummy isn't doing so well."

"Good thing Mr. Bunny brought saltines!" said Mr. Bunny.

Mrs. Bunny just threw him a look.

"All right. Let's go find the deck. The brochure suggested moonlit strolls on the deck. Even in economy," said Mr. Bunny, pulling out the brochure he kept handy in his pocket, with its map of the ship and listed activities.

Mr. and Mrs. Bunny followed signs to THE DECK. What they found when they got there was a steward with diving gear to pass out and a porthole.

"Where's the deck?" asked Mr. Bunny. Then he added, "My good man," the way he had heard people address servants in movies.

"Right out this porthole. Have to strap on an oxygen tank and some fins, of course."

"For strolling on the deck?"

"Don't so much stroll as swim. You know your deck is underwater, don't you?"

"The brochure said *MOONLIT* strolls," protested Mr. Bunny.

"Oh, they're moonlit, all right."

" 'The romance of moonlight on water,' " read Mr. Bunny from the brochure.

"Oh, the moonlight's on the water, all right. Course, you have to look *up* at it," said the steward.

"This is ridiculous," said Mr. Bunny. "When I get back to Rabbitville, I'm going to sue! I'm going to sue everyone in sight. I'm going to sue YOU, my good man." He waved the brochure in the steward's face. The steward backed up a few paces.

"Here, here," said the steward, "no need to take it out on me. I bet you bought the economy package, didn't you?"

Just then the Bunnys spied Mrs. Treaclebunny hopping back to her room from dinner.

"Oh, Mr. and Mrs. Bunny!" she said joyously, hopping up to them. "Wasn't that a delish dinner? The caviar! The lobster! The quenelles."

"You had quenelles? Oh, Mr. Bunny, I have always wanted quenelles!" cried Mrs. Bunny in anguish.

"What are quenelles?" asked Mr. Bunny.

"I don't know, but I have always wanted them," said Mrs. Bunny.

"Oh, for heaven's sakes. Listen, Mrs. Treaclebunny, stick to saltines in the stateroom, that's my advice. We saw birds pooping in the Swedish meatballs."

"Birds?" said Mrs. Treaclebunny. "Oh, of course, you're in the service where the pets are served. It's almost all bunnies at second service. A few marmots, I'm afraid, and an antelope or two, but they're really *quite* refined. I had the most interesting talk with one about her trip up the Alps. And the ship's orchestra! Divine!"

"Oh, oh, oh!" said Mrs. Bunny in agitation. "And I suppose you danced!"

"Danced? Good Lord, who wants to dance? No, there's no dancing although I hear there is up on the human deck. But the music was quite good. I tapped my toes aplenty, let me tell you."

"Oh, how I wish I could dance to the ship's orchestra. Or even just tap my toes," said Mrs. Bunny.

"Yes, Mr. Treaclebunny and I always enjoyed the music. But speaking of dancing, I should probably change and go to bunny aerobics. It starts in the gym in half an hour. They call it the Hopping Haven. Isn't that cute?"

"Mr. Bunny doesn't care for a cute gym," said Mr. Bunny. "But maybe I'll change and join you. I could lift weights. Perhaps Mrs. Bunny would like to do a little aerobicizing."

"Can't. Only for those in first class. No economy-class bunnies allowed in the Hopping Haven. I wonder if there are any chompies in my room yet? Toodle-oo."

Mrs. Bunny could no longer keep her upper lip stiff. Despite herself, tears began to roll down her furry cheeks.

"Well, how about a few more saltines!" said Mr. Bunny enthusiastically.

Mrs. Bunny's shoulders slumped as she shuffled sadly in the direction of their room. Mr. Bunny could stand it no more.

"Mrs. Bunny, I have an idea!" he said, pretending not to see that she was crying. "What if Mr. Bunny finds the head honcho and gets our tickets changed to first class?"

"Oh, Mr. Bunny," said Mrs. Bunny, grabbing his arm. "But what about your fear we will be bankrupted by this trip?"

"Well, I may have, ahem, overstated our financial situation somewhat," said Mr. Bunny.

"Oh, Mr. Bunny!" And now Mrs. Bunny's tears were for pure joy. "You always save the situation with your bunny verve and masterly ingenuity."

"Yes, those are words that describe me very well indeed," said Mr. Bunny, preening. "And let me tell you something else! That brochure promised us moonlight strolling and an orchestra, and by gosh, we will have them. Come on."

"Where are you leading me?" asked Mrs. Bunny in alarm, having to hop so quickly to keep up that she was almost falling off her strappy sandals. Mr. Bunny was moving like a bunny on a mission.

He raced ahead until he got to a large steel door. The handle was so high up it was clear that no bunnies were meant to open it, but Mr. Bunny ignored this with his masterly verve. He leapt upward, grabbed the handle and pulled down hard. The door opened. On the other side was a long staircase.

"Where does this lead?" asked Mrs. Bunny as they hopped up.

"To the human deck."

"We can't go up there. That's against the rules," said Mrs. Bunny. "And Mrs. Treaclebunny says that if they find you up there, they grab you by your ears and throw you overboard."

"Ha!" said Mr. Bunny through pants as they continued up and up and up. At last Mr. Bunny opened another door, which led outside. The Bunnys were finally topside. They took deep breaths; it was so good to finally breathe the fresh sea air. The moon glistened on the water. The deck was lovely shiny wood. In the distance they could hear an orchestra playing.

"I think I can safely say that Mrs. Treaclebunny doesn't know everything," said Mr. Bunny. "Now come on."

They strolled romantically up and down the deck a few times, watching dolphins diving through the moonlit waves, the gentle movement of constellations toward the next horizon, and feeling the soft tropical sea breezes as the ship headed south. Then, sated with loveliness, they made their way to the dining room, where second human service was still going on. Mr. Bunny hopped boldly to the bar, grabbed two glasses of champagne and brought them to the table that Mrs. Bunny was crouched under.

"Here," he said. "First the champagne, then it's your choice, dinner or dancing."

"Oh, dancing!" breathed Mrs. Bunny in delight. On the ballroom floor couples swayed and waltzed to the show tunes. All the dresses were beautiful. All the suits were divine. Jewels glittered under chandeliers. Mrs. Bunny had never seen so much sparkle all in one place. It quite took her breath away. The orchestra was playing "Wunderbar" from *Kiss Me, Kate.* It was Mrs. Bunny's favorite show tune. All Mrs. Bunny's life she had longed to waltz to "Wunderbar."

She downed the last of her champagne and then, at Mr. Bunny's bidding, threw the glass against the fireplace. Mr. Bunny had seen people do this in a movie once and had always thought it looked like fun. Several people turned their heads to the sound of tinkling glass, but no one gave it more than a passing glance in all the gaiety of the evening. Then, perhaps because the champagne had caused them to throw caution to the winds, Mr. and Mrs. Bunny, instead of dancing discreetly under the table, hopped out to the dance floor. Mr. Bunny was quite the adept waltzer, even though waltz-hopping is the most difficult sort, and he kept Mrs. Bunny turning and swaying so long that her ears twisted around each other to form one spiral. She thought she was in a dream. The music would never end, the waltz-hopping would never end, the moonlight was forever. Nobody seemed to be looking down to spy two rabbits floating enchantedly in the starlight. Until Mrs. Bunny, dreamily dipping and swaying, heard from across the dance floor:

"MR. AND MRS. BUNNY! WHAT ARE *YOU* DOING HERE?"

# ⊱MILDRED SUFFERS
# A SEA CHANGE⊰

"**I** feel that I've stumbled into a dream, a beautiful athletic-equipment-free dream," said Katherine.

After they had boarded, Katherine phoned her parents to explain everything and give them her address in England. Then the girls were sent to find the steward and change their sleeping arrangements. Originally Madeline was to sleep in Flo and Mildred's stateroom, but now they would need a separate stateroom for Katherine and Madeline.

"Why?" asked the steward, whose name tag read PERCY, looking at his cabin chart. "Why were you down as three and suddenly you're four?"

"I'm the youngest," said Katherine. "Everyone is always forgetting about me."

"The youngest, eh?" said Percy, who didn't act anything like the stewards on *Love Boat* reruns. He wasn't happy and charming and aiming to please. He looked as if he would like to throw both girls overboard at the first opportunity. "You appear to be exactly the same age as this one." He pointed to Madeline.

"I'm not. I'm younger," said Katherine. She *was* four months younger than Madeline.

"You're not even dressed like you're from the same family. You've got on some weird getup and ripped-up shoes and your pal here has got on proper cruising clothes," said Percy.

"Welcome to my world," Madeline whispered to Katherine.

"My mother taught me never to make remarks about people's clothes," said Katherine, who was coming to dislike Percy more and more.

"Oh, she did, did she," growled Percy. "Well, as long as you're on board ship, you'll be answering to me. You make sure you change into appropriate clothes. You're not paying passengers, you know. You're ship employees, as far as we're concerned. You're ambassadors for the ship, and we expect you to look and act the part."

"Oh, don't worry," said Madeline. "We're going right now to find the ship's store that sells evening wear and buy appropriate evening clothes."

"I'll worry if I want to. You look like a couple of trouble-makers to me. Just remember, one wrong move out of you and it's all up. And if I find out either one of you isn't really Flo's daughter, you'll be CHARGED for your passage. That's a two-thousand-dollar ticket, you know. And then we'll make the two of you walk the plank. Or toss you in the brig. We may be a cruise ship, but we have a brig, you know."

"I know, 'Incredible Cruises Has Everything,'" said Katherine, quoting the ship's motto, which was printed everywhere. She grabbed the key to their new stateroom and pulled Madeline away.

"Ugh," she said when she got Madeline into the hallway. "He's not exactly a barrel of laughs, is he? I don't know what a brig is, but only pirates make you walk the plank. He's just trying to scare us."

"Two thousand dollars," said Madeline. "That's pretty scary. No wonder they only let you bring family members."

"Don't worry. Some of those marimba players had about a dozen relatives with them. Your family is a cheap date by comparison."

"But if he did prove you weren't my sister, we'd have to pay for you and it would wipe out all the money Flo made from the campground."

"We'll just have to make sure we stay out of his way," said

Katherine soothingly. "He'll probably forget all about us if he never sees us again. We'll find places to hang out on shipboard where he isn't. Come on, let's go try on evening dresses. How much did Flo give you for our clothes?"

"Three hundred dollars," said Madeline. "It makes me nervous just to carry it. It's more than I have in my college education fund."

"Well, we don't have to spend all of it. We could buy the cheapest dresses and shoes they have and you could put the rest in your fund, or we could buy scissors and some needles and thread and make dresses out of our bedspreads. I bet we'd save a bundle that way."

"I think ripping up the bedspreads probably comes under the category of the 'one wrong move' Percy is just waiting for us to make," said Madeline.

"You said your mom sews," said Katherine. "Maybe we can buy some fabric on board and she can help us make dresses."

"Good idea," said Madeline. "I'm sure she's bored to death already. The only things she would be remotely interested in here are the yoga classes and marimba concerts. She'd probably love to have some sewing to do. And she'd certainly approve of our thrift. She hates spending money. She says most things should be bought recycled and secondhand and what isn't you should make or grow yourself."

The girls hunted for a store where they could get dress-making supplies. They stopped in the children's evening-wear store first but as they suspected, dresses, while wonderfully fancy, started at one hundred dollars. Shoes were even more expensive.

The girls spent the rest of the day going in and out of shops. They found scissors and needles and thread but no fabric.

"We could make them out of beach towels!" said Katherine, draping one over her shoulder to demonstrate.

"I suppose," said Madeline uncertainly. "If Mildred helps she might be able to cut them so that it's less obvious they were made out of towels. Let's go find her."

But the girls didn't have to find Mildred, for just at that second a sweet cooing voice called, "Girls, oh, girls! Isn't the shopping *divine?*"

At first Madeline didn't look up from the towels she was examining because she didn't know anyone who talked like this. But a hand dripping in gaudy rings grabbed her shoulder and spun her around, and Madeline found herself looking into the face of a platinum blonde with a strong perfume smell and too much makeup. She was wearing a gold lamé bikini with a loosely tied cover-up and some sparkling sandals. Madeline stared. Her mouth fell open.

"Well, honestly, dumpling, close your mouth before you

trip and fall in it," said the strange and yet familiar woman with a twinkling starry laugh.

"Mildred?" ventured Madeline tentatively.

"Yes?" said Mildred.

"What have you done to yourself?"

"I haven't *done* anything to myself," said Mildred. "Don't be so dramatic."

"But your hair, the jewelry, the makeup . . ." Madeline's voice trailed off. "Are you trying to fit in?" she asked, dropping her voice to a whisper. "Did Percy tell you that you have to be a ship's ambassador? Is that what this is about? We don't have to dye *our* hair, do we?"

"Ambassador? Fit in? Oh, you mean all this?" said Mildred, turning around to display her new look. "This is Cruising Mildred. This fab woman, Selma, I met at the salon who lives in Las Vegas with her husband, Tony, says that whenever she takes a cruise she gets a desire to meditate and eat nothing but fruit. She says it's her cruising self. Cruising-Fruit-Eating Selma, she calls her. Totally different from Land-Based-Criminally-Inclined Selma. It's called a sea change. It's very common. It turns out that Cruising Mildred loves to blow money. Just loves it. I haven't stopped shopping since I found out. Let me tell you, Cruising Mildred is a lot more fun than Old-Stick-in-the-Mud-Hornby-Island Mildred."

"So all this is going to stop the minute you touch land?" asked Madeline nervously.

"Maybe," said Mildred.

"We were just going to try and find you. We were hoping you could help us make some dresses from beach towels," interjected Katherine.

"Oh, for heaven's sakes, girls. *Buy* dresses. Cruising Mildred doesn't engage in menial labor like sewing. Poo. Pooey poo poo."

Cruising Mildred seemed to come with her own vocabulary. Madeline had never heard her mother say "poo."

Mildred marched over to a rack and picked the two gaudiest dresses she could find. One was purple with stripes of black sequins. The other was a strange affair that looked like a tutu with little fairy wings attached on the back. They cost two hundred dollars apiece. Mildred snatched Madeline's money out of her hand and opened her purse to unroll the wad there. She handed the money to the salesgirl. "We'll take these. Oh, and shoes." She grabbed two pairs of high heels, one covered in rhinestones, one covered in fake fur, and paid for those as well. Then she handed the bagged purchases to the girls. "Enjoy."

"Those shoes cost TWO HUNDRED DOLLARS!" shrieked Madeline.

"I know, *what* a *bargain*! Now, toodle-oo, gotta catch some

rays, and then I'm off for my aromatherapy session," said Mildred, leaving the girls outside the shop.

"Aromatherapy! Not all the activities are free. I'm pretty sure you have to pay extra for aromatherapy!" called Madeline.

"What a Debbie Downer," Mildred muttered as she sped away.

Madeline stood for a second staring at Mildred's sparkly retreating back. Then she looked down at their bags.

"Those shoes cost a fortune and they're hideous. Who wears fake-fur high heels?"

"Well . . . ," said Katherine. "It might be kind of fun—in a tacky kind of way. Remember in *Little Women* when Meg went to Vanity Fair?"

"Don't you start," said Madeline.

"What's done is done," said Katherine sensibly. "At least we'll fit in at dinner. Let's just forget it and have some fun. What's there to do here anyway?"

It turned out there was so much to do that even Madeline forgot her money worries. There were lectures to attend, and pools and movie theaters. There was even a skating rink. There were classes and games and crafts. The girls took a waltz class and started a calligraphy course.

Occasionally they ran into Mildred, always on the fly, always with more bags over her arms.

"What can she be buying?" asked Madeline. "What will she do with all this stuff when she gets home? What will Flo say?"

"Try not to think about it," said Katherine. "I'm sure she'll settle down by dinner."

But Dinner Mildred was as strange as Shopping Mildred. She was obsessed with "the best" of everything. She called the waiter *garçon* and demanded the best champagne. The best caviar. The best pork chops.

"But you're a vegan!" protested Madeline when the plate of steaming chops arrived.

"Not Cruising Mildred. Cruising Mildred loves her meaties!" said Mildred, digging in with knife and fork.

Madeline broke into a nervous sweat. She wondered if she should tell Flo so it wouldn't come as a shock when he saw her, but he was busy with the band in another part of the ship and she decided to let him stay blissfully oblivious.

Katherine looked at Madeline's worried face.

"Come on, let's dance," she said, pulling Madeline out onto the dance floor. They weren't very adept at waltzing despite their dance class, and Katherine squawked "Honk honk" when the going got tight and other couples got in their way. Soon many of the dancers, all of whom seemed to be over sixty, were steering their partners through the milieu going "Honk honk" as well.

Katherine was honking loudly when a turn around a pillar brought them right in front of Percy. He glared at the girls and said, "Did *you* start that honking?" But he was swept out of the way by an older couple who had introduced beeping as a new twist.

"Oh, Henry, I never had so much fun. Nobody honks or beeps on the *Princess* Cruises," said a beaming woman clad all in chartreuse.

"Curses!" said Percy. "The luck you have! It was going to be the brig for you for disturbing the passengers, but apparently they *like* it." He strutted off to find a waiter to chew out instead.

"We should tell him it's not luck, it's synchronicity," said Katherine.

But Madeline didn't seem to hear her. She had stopped mid–box step and squeezed Katherine's hand too tightly, hissing, "Look!"

Katherine turned her head, which caused her to fall off her fake-fur heels and onto the train of a dowager who crashed into a waiter who dropped his tray of champagne glasses. Over the ensuing chaos Katherine heard Madeline cry, "MR. AND MRS. BUNNY! WHAT ARE *YOU* DOING HERE?"

Katherine's eyes followed Madeline's to where two bunnies stood rooted in surprise.

"Are you talking to those rabbits?" asked Katherine. "The ones in *evening wear*?"

Percy heard the commotion and raced over. His eyes followed Madeline's to Mr. and Mrs. Bunny, still frozen on the dance floor.

"You brought *PETS*?" he cried. "That's *absolutely* against the rules! HA! I've got you now!"

Although Incredible Cruises had a storage area for pets, it knew nothing about the deck for animals nor the still lower one for bugs. They were run by different cruise lines altogether.

Before Madeline could disentangle Katherine from the wreckage, Percy had pounced upon the Bunnys and scooped them up by their ears. Holding one in each hand, he swiftly walked them off the dance floor.

"Oh dear, oh dear, oh dear," said Mrs. Bunny. She and Mr. Bunny had seen the steward racing toward them but were paralyzed with terror and unable to hop away in time.

"I feel this is all my fault," said Mr. Bunny as Percy carried them to the rail. "I should have reacted sooner. I was like a deer in the headlights."

"I froze too, Mr. Bunny. It was all my fault. Before we die a watery death I want you to know that I love you and I take full responsibility for our premature demise," said Mrs. Bunny.

Then she added reflectively, "Of course, you *were* the one who dragged me up to the human deck."

"*You* were the one who wanted to waltz," said Mr. Bunny. "I was perfectly happy out of sight under some table."

"Well, *you* bought the economy-class tickets."

"Well, *you* wanted to go on vacation. I was the one who said never leave the hutch."

"Are you going to tell me you anticipated being thrown overboard by your ears?"

"Well, I anticipated *SOMETHING* bad. That's more than you anticipated, Mrs. Bunny."

"This is just like you, Mr. Bunny, to start out saying it is all your fault and end up blaming me."

"*You* did that. You did that first."

"Did not."

"Did too."

"Did not."

"Did did too."

"Oh, what does that mean? It goes *double* for you?"

Both were determined to get the last word even if that last word was "glub" as they sank to the bottom of the ocean. But just then a voice called, "AH, PERCEVAL! Just the man I wanted to see!"

It was the captain. He was, Mrs. Bunny noticed, a particularly dishy captain. She'd never seen so much starch in one uniform.

"There're a lot of older passengers wanting to start a rumba line but they can't seem to organize it. They're rumbaing in six different directions and getting more and more sweaty and confused. A couple of the gentlemen are turning unnatural colors. What is the first duty of Incredible Cruises' staff?"

"Anticipate apoplexy, sir," said Percy.

"Exactly. I need you, man, to attend to this at once. Lead the rumba! Lead the rumba for God and queen!"

"Well, really, sir," whined Percy. "I am in the middle of a most important chore." He held up the Bunnys for the captain to see.

Just as he did so an earsplitting cry rent the air. Madeline and Katherine came racing up.

"You found them!" cried Madeline. "You found our stuffed animals!"

"Stuffed . . . ," spluttered Mr. Bunny. "I have been called many things, but never—"

"Hush," said Mrs. Bunny, and put on what she hoped was an amiable stuffed expression.

"Ah, excellent, Perceval. You were returning to these children their misplaced toys. Now go lead that rumba! Remember the rhythm! Tada tada DA DA!" sang the captain, doing a few rumba steps on the deck to demonstrate.

"But they're not stuffed—" began Percy.

"You see—" began Mr. Bunny.

"Hush," said Mrs. Bunny.

"I do not like to be hushed," said Mr. Bunny.

"Tada tada DA DA!" the captain sang on. "Run, Perceval! There's not a moment to be wasted! There are passengers not having their full quota of FUN!"

Percy shoved the Bunnys at the girls with the whispered warning "It ain't over till it's over" and ran to help corral the errant rumbaers. The captain tipped his hat at the girls and walked in the opposite direction. Madeline and Katherine and Mr. and Mrs. Bunny were left panting on the deck.

"That was close," said Mrs. Bunny.

"Too close," said Madeline. "But, Mr. and Mrs. Bunny, what are you *doing* here?"

"We're on vacation!" said Mrs. Bunny.

Katherine, who couldn't understand anything the Bunnys were saying, was looking a bit pale.

"This is my friend Katherine," said Madeline. "Katherine, this is Mr. and Mrs. Bunny. They understand English but they don't speak it. I understand them because it turns out I understand all animal languages."

"How?" asked Katherine.

"I don't know," said Madeline. "I just do. Uncle Runyon,

who has gone to Africa to study the language of elephants, says that there are people, like dog whisperers or horse whisperers, who naturally understand certain animals but that some very few people understand all animal languages."

"Well, I guess that's not me. It sounds like they're speaking gibberish to me," said Katherine.

"I told you we should have taken that correspondence course," said Mrs. Bunny, elbowing Mr. Bunny.

"It seems strange you never mentioned being friends with talking rabbits," said Katherine, and sat down.

"It's not an easy subject to introduce into casual conversation," said Madeline.

Mr. Bunny's fur was beginning to ruffle. "All rabbits are 'talking,'" he began testily.

"Your evening clothes are lovely," said Madeline quickly to deflect him. She had almost forgotten how sensitive to slights he was.

"I like your tuxedo!" said Katherine to Mr. Bunny, trying as best she could to make her way in these unfamiliar social waters.

"Hmmm, it is nice," said Mrs. Bunny, eyeing it critically. "But I wonder, Mr. Bunny, if we can't change it for a nice white uniform?"

"Why?" asked Mr. Bunny suspiciously.

"Oh . . . no reason," said Mrs. Bunny airily, but a little string of drool was forming on her chin as she watched the captain ascend some stairs.

"All right. Enough about clothes," said Mr. Bunny. Sometimes when he was surrounded by women, as he always seemed to be of late, he did get tired of the endless need for haberdashery chitchat. "Madeline, the important question is what are *you* doing here?"

"It's synchronicity," said Madeline. "You see, Flo found some Pop-Tarts that he thought were mystical and he decided to become the Dalai Lama of sugar and then we wanted to take a trip and he found out we could go free if his band played on board and he said it was synchronicity, that everything lined up in the stars so that the universe could attain its one ultimate good. According to him, Zanky's thirty acres for sale and my mother's organic vegetable growing and the candy store and the Dalai Lama of sugar are all connected."

Madeline took a deep breath. The Bunnys' eyes went back and forth as they tried to process all this.

Katherine added, "Except now Mildred has had a sea change and is buying everything in sight with money that should go to Madeline's college education fund but still Flo says it will all work out because of synchronicity. We just have to 'go with the flow' and 'trust the universe.'"

"Oh, Mr. Bunny!" said Mrs. Bunny. "Synchronicity. Trusting the universe."

"Stuff and nonsense," said Mr. Bunny. "Lunacy and magical thinking. And you have glossed right over the most important point completely, Mrs. Bunny. What is this about a college education fund?"

"Oh, nothing much," said Madeline, not wishing to worry the Bunnys.

Katherine was elbowing Madeline in the ribs every time the Bunnys spoke, wanting a translation. "What is he saying?" she said.

"He wants to know about the college education fund."

"Oh, well, I have one and Madeline doesn't, but she needs one more than me because she wants to grow up and be a scholar."

"Of course she should be a scholar," said Mr. Bunny.

"She would be an ace!" said Mrs. Bunny.

"An ace plus," said Mr. Bunny. "But she'll never have a college fund if she relies on those ridiculous parents and their magical thinking to provide it. It's a cruel world out there, and you have to push and claw your way to the top."

"Oh! Oh!" said Mrs. Bunny in distress. "Not so very cruel, surely, Mr. Bunny. Retract your claws! Retract your claws!"

"Torturously cruel," said Mr. Bunny with satisfaction.

"Not everywhere," said Mrs. Bunny.

"Everywhere," said Mr. Bunny, who did so like bold statements that got big reactions.

"Not on Incredible Creature Cruises, 'where anything is possible,'" said Mrs. Bunny, reading from the brochure. She was wringing her handkerchief and darting worried looks at the girls. "And not when you're in a time of synchronicity where everything works together to bring you the one ultimate good."

"Synchronicity indeed. One ultimate good indeed. Cash, Mrs. Bunny. That's what Madeline needs. Try applying to college saying you plan to pay your tuition when the synchronicity kicks in. We worked hard to put our bunnies through college. Did I leave my job at the carrot marketing board to take up skydiving because the universe wanted it? Did I go around linking breakfast sausages, new age poetry and left-handed buttonhooks in the mistaken belief they were clues to a greater good? Let us all just GET AHOLD OF OURSELVES. Madeline, Mrs. Bunny and I would help you pay for college but our money would be useless to you," said Mr. Bunny.

"Because your currency is on the gold standard," said Mrs. Bunny to Madeline.

"And ours is on the carrot standard," said Mr. Bunny, sadly shaking his head. "It wouldn't work."

"Never mind," said Mrs. Bunny. "We'll find a way for you to make money. Perhaps you can send in box tops. Mrs. Treaclebunny says that humans are always sending them in for swell prizes. Mr. Bunny once got a secret decoder ring that way, and I am still waiting for my handy-dandy ear fluffer. They say delivery in six weeks. Although so far it has been four years and seven months, but I am sure it will arrive any-time now."

"Please do not start again with the box tops. Your ear fluffer may have been only thirty-two box tops but the shipping and handling was forty-two dollars. I saw a perfectly fine ear fluffer at the drugstore for nine ninety-nine," said Mr. Bunny.

"It did not come with a flea and tick detector and a free trial-sized bottle of fur-curling lotion," said Mrs. Bunny with dignity.

Mr. Bunny turned to Katherine, wishing to include her even though Madeline had to translate. "Mrs. Bunny went to Bunnycostycost and brought home seventeen cartons of Frosted Flakes just for the box tops. She didn't even check first to see if Mr. Bunny *liked* Frosted Flakes."

"Oh well, it made excellent mulch," said Mrs. Bunny faintly. "The roses liked it, even if you did not. And besides, you may make fun of box tops, but have you a better idea?"

"Naturally I do, Mrs. Bunny. While you have been nattering

on, Mr. Bunny's big brains have been cranking it out. They cannot help themselves. Crank, crank, crank."

"That certainly is the word that comes to mind when one is around Mr. Bunny," said Mrs. Bunny quietly to herself.

"If I did not know better, Mrs. Bunny, I would think you were being unkind, but never mind," said Mr. Bunny. "Here is what my gigantic bunny brains have come up with. Organic vegetables are expensive."

"They are," said Katherine when Madeline had translated. "My mother only buys organic, and she says the stuff at the Comox farmers' market is much more expensive than the supermarket but it's worth it."

"Arrant nonsense, but never mind," said Mr. Bunny. "I have taken the disparate pieces you mentioned and put them in logical order. You are going to England because Flo and Mildred plan to make money with the candy store."

"That's right," said Madeline.

"They want to use the money to buy the thirty acres next to your own. Then Mildred will grow organic vegetables and sell them at the market."

"Yes," said Madeline.

"Which will make yet more money."

"Yes."

"What will Mildred do with the money she makes selling vegetables?"

Mr. Bunny had been pacing up and down the deck as he related all this. How it did remind him of his fine performance the time he and Mrs. Bunny were called before the Bunny Council, where his quick thinking and fine histrionics had once more saved the day.

"I don't know," said Madeline. "Until her sea change, Mildred always said money made her uncomfortable and Flo said that the crime of robbing a bank was nothing compared to the crime of founding a bank."

"He would," said Mr. Bunny. "Well, it seems to me if that is how they feel, then they would be uncomfortable keeping that organic-veggie money. They need to drop it like a hot potato. Right into your college education fund."

"OH!" said Madeline. "Oh, oh, oh!"

"Oh!" said Mrs. Bunny. "Mr. Bunny!"

"Yes," said Mr. Bunny, "for so I am called."

"You are so brilliant!"

"What have I been telling you, lo these many years?" said Mr. Bunny. "I fear, Mrs. Bunny, that you often present me to your readers in a skewed manner that does not display my giant bunny brains in their true light."

"Whatever," said Mrs. Bunny. "What you have outlined is synchronicity leading to the one ultimate good."

"Humph," said Mr. Bunny. "Not synchronicity but the logical progression of events put in an organized manner by a brain not awash in magical thinking."

"It's just a matter of semantics," said Mrs. Bunny, and then turned to the girls to discuss, with Madeline doing some swift translating, what she should wear to dinner the next night. She was thinking a flame chiffon but she realized she hadn't quite the right shoes. You needed something you could both hop and dance in.

"Yes," agreed the girls eagerly. "Shoes are always a problem."

Mr. Bunny rolled his eyes. Mrs. Bunny got out her writing notebook and scribbled:

> Poor Mr. Bunny. We must find him a male bunny pal he can hawk and spit and scratch with. Or try harder to interest him in tulle.

"What are you writing?" he asked.

"Oh, nothing," said Mrs. Bunny, putting away her notebook and giving him her most winning smile.

So Mr. Bunny got out a notebook of his own. It was full of trip expenses and had no room left to write in and the pencil he took from his pocket was missing its lead, but, thought Mr. Bunny, scribbling away with an evil smile on his face, Mrs. Bunny didn't know that.

"What are *you* writing?" asked Mrs. Bunny, looking perturbed.

"Oh, nothing, certainly no searing notes about your character," said Mr. Bunny. "Certainly not an alphabetized list of your flaws."

Mrs. Bunny started to protest but Mr. Bunny gave her his most winning smile. So they left it at that.

# LAND HO!

Madeline found it hard to keep her mind on the problem of Mrs. Bunny's shoes. For Mr. Bunny had showed her a light. A light at the end of the college-fund tunnel. Maybe the universe was appearing with help for her just when she needed it. Maybe the stars were aligning after all.

She and Katherine said good night to Mr. and Mrs. Bunny. Everyone was exhausted but vowed to meet up again the next day.

Then Mr. and Mrs. Bunny went back down to the bunny deck to find Mrs. Treaclebunny and tell her about Madeline and Katherine. They found her in the Hopping Haven, wearing a pink leotard and pink terry-cloth sweatband, aerobicizing her little heart out. She would not stop hopping no matter how frantically Mrs. Bunny waved at her to join them, so Mr. Bunny finally had to hop over and sit on her.

"Interesting variation," said the aerobics instructor, nodding enthusiastically at Mr. Bunny. "That looks excellent for core strength. Quick, everyone, hop on someone and pin them to the ground!"

There was a lot of excited commotion as all tried to be the hopper-on, not the hopped-upon.

"Talk about sloshing your brains back and forth in the cranium too much," said Mr. Bunny through gritted teeth, nodding back to the aerobics instructor while he tried to get Mrs. Treaclebunny, who kept banging her tail to the beat, to sit still.

Finally, he gave up and yanked her right out of the room.

"What did you do that for?" she complained as she panted out in the hallway with the Bunnys around her.

"Listen, you—" began Mr. Bunny, who did not like tackling sweaty bunnies when he was in formal attire.

Mrs. Bunny interrupted him. "We came to tell you about startling and exciting new developments." Mrs. Bunny clasped her hands in front of her chest in the thrilling pose of an operatic heroine. She thought this must look particularly effective in fancy dress. "Madeline is on board and so now every fiber of Mr. and Mrs. Bunny's being will no longer be directed toward Mrs. Bunny becoming queen—"

"I don't recall Mr. Bunny's fibers ever being so directed," interrupted Mr. Bunny.

"But rather toward making sure Madeline gets a college education fund. And you can join us anytime," said Mrs. Bunny generously.

"College education fund," snorted Mrs. Treaclebunny. "That's what this world needs. More useless eggheads. Now, my dear nothing-left-but-the-bones dead husband was a self-made bunny. No college education. He graduated from the eighth grade and then built his rubber empire from scratch. I cannot in all good conscience recommend anything less for your little Madeline. Tell her to pull herself up by her bootstraps. Tell her there's no time like the present for quitting school and going to work in the mines."

"Work in the mines? What mines?" said Mrs. Bunny.

"Rubber empire? He had one small rubber factory!" protested Mr. Bunny. "And speaking of mines, you have been hopping down here nonstop in Hopping Haven for hours."

"Yes," said Mrs. Bunny. "I fear any second you are going to aerobicize your brains into mush."

"Nobody likes a fat queen!" said Mrs. Treaclebunny, looking pointedly at Mrs. Bunny's new little smorgasbord belly. She had been practicing power eating at home in preparation for the trip.

Mrs. Treaclebunny flounced back into the Hopping Haven and immediately started a lot of sweaty up-and-down gyrations until two bunnies hopped on her and pinned her to the floor.

"Do you see what you started!" she called to Mr. Bunny, but her voice was drowned out by the music of the Village People.

"Oh dear," said Mrs. Bunny. "Do I look fat?"

"It is never a bad thing to take up your fair share of space," said Mr. Bunny ambiguously.

"I have been thinking, Mr. Bunny," said Mrs. Bunny. "Rather than go up north, we should perhaps go to Bellyflop, where Madeline says this candy store is. We can keep an eye on her, all the while pursuing my dream to be queen."

"I have already prepaid for the B and B up north, Mrs. Bunny. Madeline will be fine on her own. Were you not the one who said you wanted to go to the north of England to walk the moors, straining your long and fuzzy ears for the cries of 'Heathcliff! Heathcliff!'?"

Mrs. Bunny blushed. Mr. Bunny did know just how to make her sound like an idiot. "Well, perhaps we should stay in the girls' stateroom and keep an eye on them for the duration of the cruise. I did not like the way that steward was looking at them. He seemed very determined to throw us overboard even though it would clearly distress the girls."

"WHAT?" said Mr. Bunny. "Not after I just bought first-class tickets. No, Mrs. Bunny, don't even think about it. That would be pushing a bunny too far. We can certainly come up to their deck during the day to visit, but at the end of the day we retire below."

"Oh, very well," said Mrs. Bunny.

"And furthermore, if I do not take off this cummerbund soon, I will require the services of a furatologist. My fur is all mashed and sweaty."

"Yes, let us retire, Mr. Bunny. Mashed fur always makes you cranky. Perhaps Mrs. Bunny's good ideas will look better to you in the morning, when your fur has dried out."

So the Bunnys hopped off to their huge new stateroom.

"Ooooo," said Mrs. Bunny happily as they opened their door. "Chompies!"

The next few days were lovely. Mrs. Bunny had thought that bunny first-class had a lot to offer, but she almost fell over backward when Madeline handed her the list of activities on the human deck. Although Mrs. Bunny still wanted to keep one eye on the girls.

"Oh, look, Mr. Bunny, English as a Second Language. We simply *must* attend the intensive level so that Katherine will understand what we're saying. It is too awkward always having to wait for Madeline to translate."

Fortunately, the English class was next door to the girls' calligraphy. Mrs. Bunny convinced Mrs. Treaclebunny to join them. The rabbits were all hopping to the classroom together when Mrs. Treaclebunny learned that calligraphy was being offered next door. She was out of the English class like a shot.

"After all, I already speak English fluently. You have to in business," she said over her shoulder as she hopped next door. "It was many an hour that Mr. Treaclebunny, God rest his poor dead moldering paws, and I would sit about in the evening speaking a little English, a few words of Kangaroo, a little Mandarin, a touch of Thai, some Squirrel. We'd already mastered the Romance languages. But I do think I'd enjoy a spot of calligraphy."

"A spot?" said Mr. Bunny.

Mrs. Treaclebunny was starting to use a lot of British phrases. She said they crept into her speech naturally, but Mr. Bunny found this most unlikely and annoying.

"When she starts to call trucks 'lorries' and stoves 'cookers,' I shall have to take action."

"What kind of action?" asked Mrs. Bunny nervously. Mr. Bunny was unpredictable when all riled up.

"I do not know. That remains to be seen," said Mr. Bunny.

"Never mind, come hop under this chair with me, where we won't be noticed," said Mrs. Bunny. "We have a lovely view of everyone's shoes. I think you can tell so much about a person by his shoe choice, don't you?"

"More haberdashery chitchat," moaned Mr. Bunny, and then he had to be quiet as the teacher began.

When class was over, the Bunnys hopped out to meet the girls.

"There," said Mrs. Bunny, putting a paw on Katherine's knee, "now Mr. Bunny and I are fluent. We can speak like natives. And Mrs. Treaclebunny has promised to speak English from now on as well. In fact, she said when she goes to England, that's all she speaks anyway because the animals speak English there. She says anyone who has read children's books with animals in them set in England would know that. Is *The Wind in the Willows* written in Mole with a little Ratty thrown in? Is *Winnie-the-Pooh* written in Bear? No, it's English, because that's what the animals there *speak*. I didn't know that before. Travel is so broadening."

"Well, jeez, that was *fast*," said Katherine.

"Yes, I don't know why people make such a fuss about learning languages," said Mrs. Bunny vaguely, but her eye was on Mrs. Treaclebunny, who was already hopping up and down the deck poking her nose into different rooms to see what they held. All the aerobicizing had given her a very jumpy manner. She could barely sit still for two seconds at a time.

"Oh, look, the brochure says there's a cooking class in that room down the hall! I must give the teacher tips!" said Mrs. Treaclebunny, and made off for it like a shot.

"Mrs. Treaclebunny has more bossiness than brains!" said Mr. Bunny. "Did you not explain to her that while on the upper deck, it is best to hide under tables and chairs when humans are around?"

"Or try to appear stuffed. Yes, I did, but have you never tried to explain anything to Mrs. Treaclebunny?" asked Mrs. Bunny indignantly.

"Can we stop Mrs. Treaclebunny and *then* argue?" pleaded Madeline as Mr. and Mrs. Bunny squared up, facing each other.

"Good point," said Mr. Bunny.

Then they all raced into the cooking classroom.

But it was too late.

"Today we make *civet de lapin à la française,*" said the teacher. He was holding Mrs. Treaclebunny up by her ears. "My rabbits were not delivered to my kitchen today, but what luck! In hop three live replacements! And such nice plump specimens!"

"Plump! How dare you. I'm only four percent body fat," said Mrs. Treaclebunny.

But the chef wasn't listening. He raced over and grabbed Mr. and Mrs. Bunny by the ears. "First I will show you how to skin a rabbit," he said.

"Those are our pets!" said Madeline.

"They are my entrée!" insisted the chef.

"Someone call a steward," said a woman nervously. "This doesn't seem right."

A man ran into the hallway just as the chef lifted his knife.

"Don't kill me!" screamed Mrs. Treaclebunny.

"That rabbit is talking!" said another woman.

"I told you not to start the day with mai tais," said her husband.

"I heard it too!" said another woman. "That rabbit said, 'Don't kill me!' I'm a member of PETA and I'm making a citizen's arrest."

The man who had gone out to find a steward returned with Percy.

"You mustn't let this teacher kill the bunnies," said the PETA member. "They belong to those little girls."

"Yes, hand them over, François," said Percy to the teacher. "Here on Incredible Cruises we treat all animals humanely."

The teacher, with slitty-eyed bad humor, handed the three rabbits to Percy, who marched out. The girls ran after him.

Behind them they could hear François say, "We will substitute texturized soy protein, but I will not speak for the results."

"I've got you now!" said Percy as he carried the rabbits to the ship rail. "And it's overboard you go."

"Oh no, oh no!" said Mrs. Bunny. "That's not humane. That's not humane at all. Let's just throw some texturized soy protein overboard and call it a day!"

"I don't really see how this works into your theory of synchronicity, Mrs. Bunny," said Mr. Bunny acidly. "Or is this the one ultimate good you keep babbling about?"

"And I happen to know the captain is taking a nap," said Percy. "So there will be no last-minute reprieve for you."

He had the rabbits poised over the rail and was savoring the big moment when around the corner came the ship's doctor.

"Were you talking to those rabbits, Percy?" the doctor asked mildly.

"I was saying goodbye," said Percy, and laughed brutally.

"Oh dear," said the doctor. "Ship fever. It's as bad as a sea change. The brains slosh back and forth with the movement of the waves, getting bruised. Don't worry, Percy, old man, I'll recommend some time off in the infirmary. You'll like it, they have banana pudding."

"What? You think I'm crazy? Say something to the man!"

Percy ordered the bunnies. They each put on a glazed, congenial stuffed expression.

"They're not even real rabbits, man, can't you see that?" asked the doctor. "Now listen, there are movies in the infirmary. And they don't dock your pay. You can wear your pajamas all day!"

"Don't be ridiculous. Who are you signaling over? Wait a second, are you signaling *security*? I'm telling you these rabbits talk. Just ask these children!"

"They're our stuffies," said Madeline, trying to look round-eyed and innocent.

"We like to make them clothes. Some days we take our dollies out for walks and some days our stuffies," said Katherine.

"There you go," said the doctor, turning back to Percy. "Now be reasonable. Just come along for a checkup and at least discuss the matter calmly in the infirmary. We don't want to have to cause a commotion, do we?"

The security officer stood on the sidelines eyeing Percy warily.

"They've fooled you! They've fooled all of you! They pretend they can't talk and then whenever I'm alone with them, they chatter away! Take your hands off me! I'm not going to the infirmary. I'm just taking care of the ship's vermin problem. Have a good swim!" But before he had a chance to release the bunnies into the deep, the security officer yanked him away from the rail. Madeline grabbed the bunnies and she and Katherine ran to their stateroom.

"No, no!" screamed Percy as he was led away. "They *did* talk. First in gibberish and then in *English.* And they understood everything I said too!"

"We've a nice, private room for you without any bothersome talking bunnies," said the doctor. "The only person you'll have to talk to is a nice, nice *special* kind of doctor. You can eat pudding together!"

Madeline and Katherine and the bunnies collected themselves in the girls' stateroom.

"Saved by the bell," said Mrs. Treaclebunny.

"All goes as it was meant to, synchronistically speaking," said Mrs. Bunny, but she did not push it. It had been a trying day.

"Are you all right?" Katherine asked Mrs. Treaclebunny, who was looking very upset.

"It's very unsettling," said Mrs. Treaclebunny, looking at her paws.

"It's your own fault," said Mr. Bunny. "Did we not explain how to *hide* from humans? It's true they seldom look down, but there's no sense blatantly calling attention to yourself like that."

"No, not that. I mean my paws! They're covered in ink! That calligraphy course had no fur guards at all! I shall complain to someone high up. Failing that, I shall complain to everyone in sight!"

Mr. Bunny pulled at his ears. Learning how to stay invisible to humans was an art that Mrs. Treaclebunny seemed to have no interest in learning. He feared eventually it would land them all in trouble.

"I think we need some quiet R and R," said Mrs. Bunny.

So they all got lemonades and books and spread out on deck chairs. Everyone agreed they had had quite enough excitement and had better rest before England, so this was how they spent most of their time for the remainder of the cruise. With Percy in the infirmary they had no need to hide.

For days they lolled about on deck chairs reading and doing crossword puzzles and the like. The girls tanned and the bunnies warmed their fur. When anyone approached, the bunnies glazed their eyes and looked stuffed. Nobody gave them a second glance.

"You're even reading in English now," said Katherine admiringly one day to Mrs. Bunny, who had *War and Peace* propped up on her tummy. It was a very thick book.

Mrs. Treaclebunny glanced over at Mrs. Bunny's book. "Of course, *I* read it in the original Russian. It was tip-top!"

"*Tip-top?* Grrr," said Mr. Bunny.

Mr. Bunny was about to go for another round of fruity umbrellaed drinks to keep from throttling Mrs. Treaclebunny when Madeline sat up stiff as a board and pointed. "LOOK! LAND!"

"Oh no," said Mrs. Bunny. "Our time with you cannot be coming to an end so soon!"

"Oh, Mrs. Bunny. Oh, Mr. Bunny!" said Madeline, giving each of them a hug. "We must go and finish packing. I knew we were debarking today but I didn't think we'd see land so soon. Please try to come to Bellyflop to visit."

"We will try!" said Mrs. Bunny.

"We make no promises," said Mr. Bunny. "Train fare is outrageous. Why, the fare alone between London and—"

But he was drowned out by the captain announcing that they would dock before long.

"Come, Mrs. Bunny, we must hop!" said Mr. Bunny, and the last goodbyes were lost in the sea of feet rushing to their rooms.

# ⇥STRANDED!⇤

Madeline and Katherine soon joined Flo and Mildred, who were preparing to disembark. Getting everything off the ship was a nightmare, with Mildred racing back and forth, having forgotten this or that "dear little thing" she had bought and left in the stateroom by mistake. Finally, they seemed to have all the luggage and shopping bags in one huge pile on the dock in Tilbury, the port outside London where they had landed.

"How are we going to get all this on the bus?" asked Madeline.

Suddenly Mildred's face changed. It was as if she were awakening from a dream.

"What am I doing with alpha hydroxy anti-aging cream?"

she asked, peering into one of the shopping bags. "In fact, what am I doing with all this junk? Girls, help me get rid of it."

It took a little while to distribute the bags among the homeless and then, with a lightened load, they made their way to the bus station. Madeline breathed a sigh of relief that Cruising Mildred had been left on board ship with Cruising-Fruit-Eating-Criminally-Inclined Selma.

"Everyone pick up a suitcase and let's grab that bus," said Flo, who had bought four tickets. They climbed on and, with a lurch, they were off to London.

"We'll change there for a train to Bellyflop," said Flo.

They all nodded sleepily. It was early evening but they were tired from the day's excitement and trying to find their land legs again.

The evening light dimmed as they drove into London's bright city sparkle.

"Where do we get off?" asked Mildred in bewilderment as the bus jerked to a halt at various stops. The driver called out the names of the stops but none of them could make out what he said through his thick Cockney accent.

"This is harder than trying to understand Rabbit," said Katherine.

Even Madeline, who understood all animal languages, could make neither head nor tail of it.

Flo had a map open and was reading it sideways and up-side down. "I should be able to figure out where to get off," he said. "Victoria Station is here on the map somewhere, I'm sure."

Finally, when they were the only ones left on the bus, the driver called out something that sounded like "Rylbrzmsem."

"Excuse me, did you just call out Victoria Station?" asked Madeline.

"Frezzle drom mz," said the driver.

"Close enough," said Flo, and hustled them all up and forward.

They yanked their luggage from the overhead rack at the front and raced down onto the rainy pavement.

There they stood looking left and right.

In front of them was a huge building with giant pillars. "That *must* be Victoria Station," said Flo.

They followed the mass of people moving up the steps into the giant building. But once inside they had a great deal of trouble finding the trains. Instead there were winding hall-ways and staircases.

"There're lots of mummies and such," said Madeline, peer-ing into different rooms. "But I don't see anything resembling public transport."

"What are these booklets? Train schedules?" asked Mildred,

grabbing one from a desk and reading it. "This isn't Victoria Station, Flo. This is the British Museum."

"Cool," said Flo.

A guard happened by and spied them walking along, toting their suitcases. "Moving in?" he asked jovially.

"Ha ha," said Mildred, who was very tired. "If you people weren't so hard to understand, we wouldn't be here. We'd be where we want to be."

"Where do you want to be?" asked the guard.

"Victoria Station. Could you give us directions?" asked Madeline.

"The cabby will know the way, miss," said the guard. "You'll want a cab. It's too far to walk." He tipped his hat and dashed off to keep a pair of boys from climbing on the statues.

"All right, let's get a cab," said Flo. "You'll have to pay, Mildred. The bus tickets from Tilbury ate everything in my wallet."

"Me?" said Mildred. "I don't have any money."

"Well, where's our stash? You didn't leave it under the mattress, did you? You said you'd be in charge of the cash."

"Ummm, it may be gone," said Mildred slowly. "You know, it's all coming back to me kind of mistily, the sea journey, the Donna Karan separates. . . ."

"You spent *all* of it?" squawked Madeline.

"Well, Cruising Mildred did, to be more accurate," said Mildred, looking away.

"Why didn't you tell us before this?" asked Flo.

"I wasn't keeping track," said Mildred. "Cruising-Shopping Mildred doesn't think about money."

"Well, now what do we do?" asked Flo.

"Maybe you should have thought of that before. Maybe you should have told me at Tilbury we were down to our last fifty dollars," said Mildred.

"ME?" said Flo.

Madeline could feel a fight brewing. She didn't mind so much for herself, she was feeling as crabby as everyone else, but she didn't want Katherine put in an awkward position. "Oh, have some lavender essential oil," she said, getting it out of her purse and flinging droplets about.

A family of tourists walking by stopped to watch. The father said, "Are you part of an exhibit? Is this one of those interactive museum experiences I've read about? Are we supposed to ask you about that oil? Is this some ancient rite? Just tell us what roles to play, we're keen to join in. Are you ancient Egyptians?"

"No, we're just modern Canadians," said Katherine.

"OH!" said the mother. "I've always wanted to see one of those. Harry, take a picture!"

Mildred growled slightly.

"Oh, listen to the sounds they make! I TOLD you to bring the video camera, Harry."

The family stayed rooted, waiting to see what Mildred would do next, so Madeline shuffled Katherine, Mildred and Flo into the next room.

"So!" she said when they were sure the tourists hadn't followed. "We have no money at all? We're stuck at the British Museum, which must be about ready to close, with no money and no place to stay? How are we ever going to get to Belly-flop? *What are we going to do?*"

Meanwhile, Mr. and Mrs. Bunny were on a train, trundling happily if somewhat overtiredly through the English countryside, all their bunny currency intact.

"What a lovely country," said Mrs. Bunny rhapsodically. "How it does put me in mind of the poets. *I wandered lonely as a cloud . . . ,*" she began.

"Mrs. Bunny, please tell me you're not going to declaim all through Europe," said Mr. Bunny in the crabby way of overtired travelers everywhere.

"Humph," said Mrs. Bunny. "We are not going 'all through Europe,' and I have been waiting to declaim in England for a good long while. The least you could do is lend me your bunny ears."

"If you ask me, this place hasn't got a nickel on the hutch and our own backyard. Not a wooden nickel's worth better than the Cowichan Valley, a valley of mild and temperate climate."

"And how lovely to be on land again in such countryside after our long sea voyage." The crabbier Mr. Bunny became, the more Mrs. Bunny was driven to rhapsodic crescendos.

"Lovely to be on land if the land would stay still. Ever since I got off that boat my legs have been trying to keep the earth from rolling about so."

"Oh, that's just your sea legs. They'll go away," said Mrs. Bunny airily. "I can't wait to see our B and B. Isn't this country-side like a storybook, Mrs. Treaclebunny?"

But Mrs. Treaclebunny had earlier used the three idioms "all my eye and Peggy Martin," "cor, blimey!" and "for don-key's years" all in the same sentence, proving that her Briti-cisms were picking up speed now that she was in England, and Mr. Bunny may have bitten her just a bit. Mrs. Treaclebunny had flounced out and found a whist tournament in the club car and had no plans to return anytime soon.

Oh well, thought Mrs. Bunny. She gazed out again on the emerald fields. "Can't you just not wait to see our B and B?"

"Won't have the three-hundred-thread-count cotton sheets I have at home, I bet," said Mr. Bunny gloomily. "And I like my own shower at the end of the day. Not some foreign contraption."

Mrs. Bunny gave up then and just recited poetry quietly to herself. She hoped Mr. Bunny would be in a better mood after a fine English dinner and a good night's sleep.

It was dark when they finally got to MacRabbitville in North Yorkshire. Mr. Bunny grabbed his and Mrs. Bunny's luggage. Mrs. Treaclebunny joined them and handed hers to Mr. Bunny too.

"I hope this is a good accommodation," said Mrs. Treaclebunny.

"Oh, it is. It got many fine reviews in *The International Bunny* and *Condé Rabbit Traveler*. And it's very close to the train station—we can hop right over," said Mrs. Bunny.

Mrs. Bunny and Mrs. Treaclebunny hopped out of the train and along the village sidewalk, but Mr. Bunny, who was dragging three suitcases, did not so much hop as shuffle. He was even more crabby and sweaty when he arrived at their bunny accommodations.

But when they saw it, their jaws dropped.

"This can't be right," said Mrs. Treaclebunny. "There's no B and B sign or even a card in the window."

"One whole side of the building looks collapsed," said Mr. Bunny.

"But it's the right address," said Mrs. Bunny, checking and double-checking her computer printout.

Mrs. Bunny and Mrs. Treaclebunny stood for five minutes without moving, as if the door would open on its own. Finally, Mr. Bunny let go of the luggage, hopped up to the door and banged away on its heavy knocker.

"Oh, look at that charming knocker," sang Mrs. Bunny. "It's probably been there since the time of the medieval rabbits."

There was a long silence. They could hear no one coming to the door.

Mr. Bunny knocked again. This time he might have even kicked the door a little. Finally, a very grumpy bunny in a long gown and nightcap and carrying a candle opened the door.

Perhaps, thought Mrs. Bunny, this proprietress would whip up some toad-in-the-hole or other tasty native fare and sit them in front of a roaring fire. But no, she did not look the sort. Her eyes were very slitty and mean.

"WHAT?" demanded the proprietress bunny, angrily staring at them through particularly menacing-looking spectacles.

"Oh, look at her nightcap! And the candle! No electricity! Oh, this is just so full of picturesque charm! It has all the culture shock I was wishing for and more!"

"Mrs. Bunny, if you wax rhapsodic again, I'm going to throw your suitcase into the Thames," said Mr. Bunny. "This is not the time for sensitive travelogues. Madam, we have a reservation. Show her your receipt, Mrs. Bunny."

So Mrs. Bunny did.

"Tough toenails, ducky," said the proprietress. "We're closed."

"CLOSED?" said Mrs. Bunny. "But I prepaid."

"Yeah, well, we had a fire two nights ago. Got no rooms left to let. Fire destroyed the whole guest wing."

"But I prepaid!" said Mrs. Bunny again.

"Can't help that. Act of God."

"Now see here, my good woman," said Mrs. Treaclebunny. "You owe us two rooms or a refund."

"If it's a refund you want, you'll have to wait for the insurance money to come through. In the meantime, as I already made plain, we got no rooms. Burnt to a crisp, they have."

"Well, can't you find us a room somewhere else in town?" asked Mrs. Treaclebunny.

"There aren't none. What do you think this is, America, with Holiday Inns on every corner? You'll have to go to another town. I'm going to bed."

"We're not from America, we're from *Canada*," said Mrs. Treaclebunny. "You and I share the same queen."

"Don't know what the queen's got to do with it, never had no use for her meself," said the woman, and slammed the door in their faces.

"Well!" said Mildred. "This is a fine how-do-you-do."

"Let's think, let's think," said Madeline, beginning to fidget and pace. She didn't mind being stranded like this so very much for herself. In fact, it was *just* the sort of situation she would expect to find herself in on a trip that Flo had arranged. But she minded terribly for Katherine, who was used to somewhat normal people. "What can we do? Surely there must be something we can do."

"We've got to trust in the same force that brought us the mystical Pop-Tarts," said Flo.

"Those Pop-Tarts were not mystical," said Madeline. "They were—"

"Even I would feel better if we had a plan," Mildred interrupted.

"I do have a plan," said Flo.

"Well, thank goodness," said Mildred as they all turned to him expectantly.

Flo had taken the brochure from Mildred and was flipping through it. "I'm going to check out the British Museum. This place looks really cool. And it's FREE!"

The others didn't know what to do, so they tripped dispiritedly after him, still wheeling their suitcases along.

They were so tired that only Flo was able to focus on the exhibits. The rest of them followed him mutely.

They had been there an hour when Madeline said to Katherine, "I guess synchronicity is a crock. I guess there's no big universal plan or we wouldn't be stuck here. I'm sorry you got dragged along. This is just another idea that Flo and Mildred didn't plan properly."

"But there's been a charming lack of sports equipment," said Katherine politely.

"You know, I wish I knew more about all this stuff," Flo said as they went up one aisle of exhibits and down the next. "Wait a second, there's a tour over there. Let's join it."

"I think you have to pay for those tour guides," said Madeline. "We can't just glom on."

But Flo had already edged his way into the group.

"These may look like bookcases," the tour guide was saying. "But in reality they are doors. If we open them we find secret passageways that run through the museum. Passageways that only special museum personnel are allowed to use. I'll open one for us to take a quick look but we mustn't enter."

The guide opened one of the bookcase doors.

Madeline gasped.

Standing there was the last person she expected to see.

# UNSTRANDED!

It was dark and rainy on the sidewalk. The rabbits stood in disbelief as their fur dripped on the pavement.

"Well!" said Mrs. Treaclebunny at last. "This is the last trip I let *you* plan."

"Hasn't any use for the queen!" said Mrs. Bunny. Her fur stood on end. Her claws popped out.

"Down, Mrs. Bunny," said Mr. Bunny mildly.

"I suppose we'd better take the train back to London," Mrs. Bunny said uncertainly, retracting her claws. "If there is one. There's sure to be a room in London somewhere. I'll just check my *Condé Rabbit* for a recommendation."

"No, thank you," said Mrs. Treaclebunny. "That's the last *Condé Rabbit* recommendation I believe *I'll* be using."

"To be fair," said Mrs. Bunny, "that proprietress bunny can hardly be blamed for having a fire in her B and B. And *Condé Rabbit* can't be responsible for such things."

"To be fair to *us,*" said Mr. Bunny, "and we are the only bunnies I care to be fair to just at the moment, that proprietress bunny *can* be blamed for not even offering to assist us in finding somewhere else to stay. The least she can do is let us use her phone to make alternate plans."

"Yes, knock on the door. Knock on it as hard as you can!" said Mrs. Treaclebunny. "Rouse her from her sleep and make her help us out."

"Oh dear," said Mrs. Bunny faintly. "I do so hate to bother sleepy bunnies. . . ." But it was too late. Mr. Bunny was pounding on the door for all he was worth.

It opened to an extremely irate proprietress bunny. "What's all this then? YOU? I thought I'd gotten rid of you."

"We need to make some phone calls," said Mr. Bunny.

"The well-prepared traveler always carries a cell phone," said the proprietress, sniffing.

"I do not care to stand out here in the rain arguing the point," said Mr. Bunny, storming in with Mrs. Bunny in tow. "We need to make other arrangements and we need your phone to make them."

"All right, but hurry up. I was about to have a nice hot

bath. It's quite the shock I've had today. First a fire and then foxes."

"Foxes?" said all three bunnies, dropping their suitcases in alarm.

"Yeah. Foxes, all right. Was minding me own business. Next thing I know, me guesthouse is burnt down and there's foxes scurrying about."

"Did the foxes set the fire?" asked Mrs. Bunny.

"Never thought of that," said the proprietress bunny, who, perhaps, was not the brightest carrot in the bunch. "But now that you mention it, they was carrying gasoline cans and matches, some of them."

"Of course they set the fire," said Mr. Bunny. "Foxes are the same the world over. They're no-goodniks through and through. My good woman, please bring us a phone book and phone."

"Got nothing better to do . . . wanted me bath . . . vexin'- enough day it were without demanding bunnies showin' up on me doorstep," muttered the proprietress bunny, shuffling off. "Next thing you know, they'll be asking for a pomegranate, some Marmite, a jellyfish."

"Perhaps you've had previous acquaintance with Mrs. Treaclebunny," muttered Mr. Bunny. "Now I shall call around and see if I can find us a room somewhere else."

"But where?" moaned Mrs. Bunny, who was beginning to come undone with all the stress and fatigue of the day. "We don't even have a train schedule."

"Getting a train schedule is the least of our problems," said Mr. Bunny as the proprietress returned with a phone and silently handed it to him. She escorted them back outside, then marched back inside to run her bath.

"All I wanted was to become QUEEN. Was that too much to ask?"

"I suppose we could stay in a castle," said Mrs. Treaclebunny ponderingly. "That would be safe from foxes and fires, at least."

"Yes, yes, one with big towers and dungeons. Will you get ahold of yourself, Mrs. Treaclebunny, and stop talking nonsense. It's bad enough one of you wanting to become queen without the other deciding she needs a castle," said Mr. Bunny. "We must make a practical plan, and soon. After all, if there are foxes about, I'd just as soon not hang out on this doorstep forever."

"Here," said Mrs. Treaclebunny, "give me the phone. While the two of you 'make a practical plan,' I will just call my cousin and have her pick me up. If you want to tag along, fine, or if by then you have a better 'practical plan,' do let me know."

"You have a cousin?" said Mrs. Bunny.

"Here in England?" said Mr. Bunny.

Mrs. Treaclebunny didn't even bother responding. She was busy dialing. Then chatting. Finally, she hung up. "All right then. My cousin has sent her driver for us. He should be here in an hour. She said we could stay with her. Not that it's such a great place to stay. Damp. Full of wet hedges."

"Mrs. Treaclebunny, you have saved the day," said Mrs. Bunny.

"I always say travelers must be content, don't I, Mrs. Bunny?" said Mr. Bunny, pounding Mrs. Treaclebunny gratefully on the back and trying to imagine what kind of hutch was full of wet hedges. A greenhouse-type hutch, perhaps?

"Well, he always says something," said Mrs. Bunny in the effusive way of travelers who have almost been stranded bedless and then saved.

"Any hutch in a storm," said Mr. Bunny.

"There he goes again!" said Mrs. Bunny, beaming fondly. "Mr. Bunny is nothing if not handy with an aphorism!"

"Well, it's not a hutch, that's the thing," sighed Mrs. Treaclebunny. "The last time I stayed there I said, never again. It's cold and drafty and it doesn't have granite countertops or recessed lighting. But I suppose it will have to do."

The proprietress had filled her tub and returned for the phone. "Are we all done now?" she asked acidly.

"Yes, we have been saved!" Mrs. Bunny told her rhapsodically.

"Yeah, I'm chuffed to bits, ducky," said the proprietress, and slammed the door.

The bunnies huddled under the overhang shivering until the lights of a Rolls-Royce appeared and a uniformed driver came out to load their luggage.

"Mrs. Treaclebunny!" he said warmly. "Welcome back. And how is Mr. Treaclebunny?"

"Toast."

"I'm sorry to hear it."

"Well, we all have to go sometime, Charles. Have you got any chompies back here?" she asked as the bunnies climbed into the car.

"Yes, madam, slide the door on the cabinet there. And plenty of hot chocolate."

"Excellent. Drive on," said Mrs. Treaclebunny grandly as she passed around steaming mugs of cocoa.

The bunnies sipped and nibbled. As the journey was long, they snoozed a bit on the big comfortable seats until the car jerked and rumbled over a wooden bridge. Mrs. Treaclebunny slept on but the Bunnys' eyes snapped open.

"Where are we?" whispered Mrs. Bunny.

"I don't know," said Mr. Bunny, looking into the dark rain. "But I think we're going over a . . . *moat*."

"Uncle Runyon!" yelled Madeline in alarm. The tour turned and stared at her and her family. "What are YOU doing here?"

The tour guide was so startled that she let go of the secret bookcase door and it banged closed. When she opened it again Uncle Runyon was gone. Madeline ran past the people on the tour and, before the guide could stop her, disappeared up the stairs behind the hidden door.

"HEY!" yelled the guide. "You can't go up there!"

Flo and Mildred and Katherine tried to follow, but the tour guide had by then recovered herself and slammed the door.

"Museum workers only."

"But my daughter just went there," said Mildred. "And Uncle Runyon. Practically my entire family is up there."

"You're well-enough represented, then. The rest of you can just stay put." The guide folded her arms over her chest and looked quite fierce. And then they were all shuttled out of the way by a German tour guide and a group of German tourists, several of whom kicked Flo's and Mildred's suitcases aside to get a better vantage point, despite the fact that they were still holding on to them.

Flo and Mildred waited patiently for all the tour groups to

move on. Once they had left, Flo grabbed the hidden doorknob and tried to turn it. But the door was locked and wouldn't budge.

Meanwhile, Madeline ran up the stairs as fast as she could. She could just see the back of Uncle Runyon's balding gray head as it whipped around corners. He went into a room marked COINS and the door clanged shut behind him.

Madeline tried knocking gently on the coin room door, but when no one answered she slowly opened it and entered. She was in a room with millions of little drawers with little drawer pulls. There were offices all about, opening onto the room with the coins, and at long tables men and women slumped over books and old coins, studying them and writing furiously. And at the end of a long table, writing most furiously of all, sat Uncle Runyon.

There was not a sound in the room. Madeline crept gently up and whispered, "UNCLE RUNYON!"

"Shhh, I beg you, shhh," said Uncle Runyon.

"Why aren't you in Africa studying the language of elephants?" she asked, for this was where he was headed when last she saw him.

"Because I'm in the British Museum studying coins," said Uncle Runyon, glancing nervously around.

"Why?" asked Madeline.

"Because they don't keep elephants at the British Museum."

"No, why are you *at* the British Museum? Why are you in London? Why aren't you in Africa?"

"It's a long story. We can't talk here. Can you and your family meet me in the Court Restaurant in ten minutes? I have to put this stuff away."

"All right," whispered Madeline. "We can sit with you but we can't order anything. We haven't any money. In fact, we're stranded here because we have no money whatsoever."

"Well, now, why doesn't that surprise me? What have Mildred and Flo been up to?"

"That's a long story too," said Madeline.

"All right, we'll exchange long stories in the restaurant. And you needn't worry about money. I've got plenty of it. I'm bleeding the stuff. Order what you like. I'll pay for it. And order cornflakes for me. The British are the nastiest cooks imaginable. You wouldn't believe what they eat. Toad-in-the-hole. Sticky toffee pudding. Bubble and squeak. Butler's deviled kidneys. *Luxury* toad-in-the-hole. That's where they give you extra amphibians, I guess. All the visiting scholars live on cornflakes."

Madeline made her way back to Flo and Mildred and Katherine and they trooped up to the Court Restaurant, where they ordered large meals. Without any money, who knew when they would eat again?

"Well, well, here we all are," Uncle Runyon said jovially when he'd joined them. He seemed much more relaxed than he had in the coin room. "So, you first. What are you all doing here?"

Flo told their story, complete with his theory of synchronicity.

"And you see, I told Mildred to trust the universe. Trust the universe and where does it lead us? To the British Museum, where Uncle Runyon can lend us the train fare. The stars are aligned, man. They're *aligned*!"

"Yes, yes, interesting things, stars," said Uncle Runyon, pouring seven packets of sugar on his cornflakes. "You know, of course, that they shine because of nuclear fusion at their center. Well, of course also because their gravitational energy is set free. When the hydrogen gives out, the stars can't continue with their nuclear fusion, but even after fourteen billion years of the universe's existence, this hasn't happened. Of course—"

"Yes, way cool," interrupted Mildred. "But the thing is, Uncle Runyon, as Flo said, we need to borrow some money."

"I'll give you the train fare to Bellyflop, no problem. But you mustn't speak to anyone about me or tell them that I was a decoder or studying animal languages. People will question what I'm doing here. To be honest, *I* don't really know what I'm doing here. I mean, I know what I'm doing here, it's just that it is very odd that I'm here doing it."

"You're not making any sense," said Mildred.

"It's synchronicity," said Flo staunchly.

"Yes, Flo," said Uncle Runyon irritably. "By that I assume you mean you're having a great deal of luck. But you might ask yourself if things were so synchronistic, why Mildred blew all that money to begin with. Wouldn't it have been easier for the universe to simply arrange that she hold on to your money? If things were so synchronistic, why are you stranded here with no money?"

"We're not. You're here. I know you're, like, a scientist, man. And scientists figure they gotta find things out themselves, they gotta know everything. But I don't have to find things out because I figure, you know, more will be revealed," said Flo placidly, eating his salad. "Is this union lettuce?"

"How *did* you end up here?" asked Katherine.

"Ah! Good question," said Uncle Runyon, spooning up more cornflakes. "Well, you see, I was busy studying the elephant language, making great headway. Fascinating creatures, and I *thought* they liked me. They seemed to not mind me hanging out with them. I thought we were becoming if not exactly interspecies pals, at least interspecies amiable acquaintances.

Unfortunately, when I got a certain degree of fluency, I began to understand some of their conversations, and that was when I realized that in fact they didn't like me at all. Their name for me was BIGPOOEYWHITEGUY. They were trying to decide which night to knock down my camp and trample me to death. I was shocked. I thought they had pacifist leanings. Anyhow, after deciding to trample me to death, they went on to plan the total destruction of the archaeological dig nearby. They didn't like this archaeologist, they didn't like that one. They didn't like anyone. They were extremely crabby elephants. They had politicized their crabbiness, as so often people do, and had started a coalition called Africa for Elephants.

"Well, I sneaked away to warn the archaeologists one night when I thought the elephants were sleeping, but as I got to their camp I saw a bunch of irate elephants already knocking down the dig and chasing the archaeologists in circles. I don't like to generalize, but as a whole, I would have to say that scientists—more endurance runners than sprinters. When the elephants spied me, they started racing after me. They said they didn't *want* to be studied. They didn't *want* to be understood. They liked their privacy. They thought it was cheeky of me invading their territory and eavesdropping on their conversations.

"I ran through the jungle. I could feel their hot elephant

breath on my neck. Just when I thought I was a goner, I spied one of the archaeologists' trucks with crated artifacts, getting ready to be shipped off somewhere, and without thinking I jumped in a crate just as the truck pulled away. It wasn't terribly comfortable but it was more comfortable than being under the elephants' feet. A while later the truck stopped somewhere and they hammered lids onto all the crates. But they never noticed me.

"It was cozy enough in my crate. I must have slept for hours, and the next thing I knew, I heard the roar of engines. From the freezing cold I deduced that I'd been transferred into the cargo hold of an airplane. But flying off to where? I slept more and when I awoke I was somewhere warm and silent. I kicked the lid off the crate and there I found myself in the British Museum all alone in the middle of the night. I used the washroom and raided the cafeteria's fridges and finally fell asleep in the coin room.

"The next morning I awoke with a start because people were coming and taking coins out of drawers and sitting at desks and tables, writing about them. I didn't know what else to do, so I just took some coins out of the drawers and looked like I was studying them too. I've known enough eggheads to know that they never notice anything that isn't six feet long and shoved up their nose, and indeed no one questioned my being there. I stole some paper and pens and some of their coin books and a laptop that was just lying about, and all day I pretended to be studying coins. My idea was to leave later and get Jeeves to wire me some money."

"Where was Jeeves?" asked Madeline.

"Who is Jeeves?" asked Katherine.

"My butler. He came to Africa with me but the climate didn't agree with him. It made him rashy. So I sent him home. And a good thing. He was more useful to me there. Jeeves is always good in a crisis. I figured I'd settle into a hotel and get some money and fly home. But as soon as I stepped outside the British Museum I was attacked by squirrels."

"Squirrels?"

"London's full of them, and they're nasty buggers, let me tell you. At first I thought they must be attacking everyone but soon I realized it was only me. They were *targeting* me. Let me tell you, you don't know terror until you've been targeted by squirrels. They were gathering for vicious organized assaults with acorns. Somehow they *KNEW*. The elephants must have sent them a message! They'd started a worldwide animal vendetta! I mean, the whole thing would make a fascinating paper if I could gain some objectivity, but I'm afraid every time I think about it, it just makes me mad as a hornet. Squirrels are bad enough—suppose some of the bigger animals

come after me? Dogs, for instance. Dogs can be very fierce. Or gerbils. Good Lord, you don't want to start annoying gerbils. I had to beat a hasty retreat back to the museum. And here I am."

"Oh, Uncle," said Madeline. "Are you sure the squirrel attack was really related to the elephants? Are you in fact sure you were attacked by squirrels at all? I mean, how could the elephants possibly have told the squirrels?"

"Oh yes, oh yes, you take the layman's point of view. Most people, I'm afraid, are unaware of the deep connections between living things. Did you know that an aspen grove is not a bunch of separate trees but one living organism? If you could see beneath the ground you'd find all the trees connected by a root system. And even trees not so connected *talk* to each other. And not in some *Wizard of Oz,* mean-apple-tree way. When some infestation is upon a tree it increases its tannin production to make itself taste bad so it will be left alone by caterpillars or whatnot. And it releases a chemical that tells other trees that an attack is under way so they can step up their tannin production.

"People try to replicate this kind of unspoken communication using technology because they don't trust that it really exists. They don't obey their instincts.

"In parts of Africa a visitor has been known to set out to

travel from tribe to tribe, none of whom have any modern communication devices, only to find that when he arrives, he was expected. Somehow his arrival has been communicated in advance. But how? So we make Facebook and Twitter and all those silly devices, which we then rely on, and lose the ability we had to communicate without them. It's the same with global navigational devices. People who use them lose the part of the brain that navigates naturally. We are evolving ourselves right out of our natural skills. We are giving them away to electronics. So don't tell me about elephants and squirrels."

"Yes, I'm sure you're right," said Madeline hastily. Once Uncle Runyon got started on a new theory, it was hard to deflect him. "But can't you just go home now? I mean, Jeeves could find a way to get you past the squirrels, couldn't he?"

"Oh, yes indeed. Jeeves came with a trunkload of ideas, starting with a mailbag, which I was to climb into and he, dressed as a postman, was to leave the museum carrying over his shoulder."

"The squirrels wouldn't know it was you?"

"Well, his reasoning was that they might, but they would say to themselves, 'The mail must go through!'"

"And it didn't work?"

"Well, that is where the story takes a twist. I didn't actually try it because, you see, it took him a little while to get to England, and while I was waiting I went back to the coin room and pretended to study coins again, like everyone else, but the thing is, I began to get interested. Fascinating things, ancient coins. And, well, I began to have theories. And I began to share them with the others, who encouraged me to apply for grants, and by gosh, I got them. First one, then another— everyone was sending me money. Hundreds and hundreds and thousands of pounds. To study more coins and come up with more theories. And before I knew it I was hooked. Anything you begin to study in depth can grab you. It's all so terribly interesting."

"What is?" asked Katherine.

"Everything. Everything, dear. Every little thing. Now I sleep in the coin room and use the washroom down the hall and eat in the museum's restaurant and cafés. It's really not such a bad life, so long as they keep cornflakes in stock. Fascinating things, coins."

"Well, isn't that interesting," said Mildred, yawning. "But can we get back to the subject of train fare before the last train for Bellyflop departs?"

"Right," said Uncle Runyon, and pulling out his wallet, he passed them a thick wad of money.

"Thank you," they all said, rising from the table and heading for the door.

"Goodbye, Uncle. We'll be in Bellyflop if you need us," said Madeline.

As they left the restaurant, Madeline turned and surveyed her uncle. He had gotten himself some more cornflakes and was eating them while reading a journal about coins. He had a cornflake stuck to his nose. Then she noticed that the restaurant was full of scholars, reading journals with cornflakes stuck to various bits of them. She was no longer so sure about becoming a scholar.

"Remember, man," called Flo, "you're here because of the stars!"

"I'm here," said Uncle Runyon, without looking up from his journal, "because of the squirrels."

# ⇥THE SWEET SHOPPE⇤

The Bunnys and Mrs. Treaclebunny were so exhausted when they arrived at the castle that they hardly registered anything except the maids showing them to their rooms. Mrs. Bunny said sleepily to Mr. Bunny, "This castle has very big furniture. I shall have to do a major hop to get into that bed."

And Mr. Bunny, who had already hopped beneath the heavy tapestry covers, replied drowsily, "A major mighty hop." And immediately began to snore.

In the morning, after a sound twelve-hour snooze, Mrs. Bunny awoke full of curiosity about where they were. She pushed open the shutters and such a sight met her eyes! The English countryside, just as she'd imagined it, rolling out greenly in all directions.

"Oh, Mr. Bunny!" she exclaimed, hopping back on the bed and lifting his head up by his ears so he could see out the window. "We're in a *castle*. And *look*!"

"Ow," said Mr. Bunny. "How many times do I have to tell you—I do not like being awoken by having my ears pulled."

Before he could say more there was a knock at the door and a very odd-looking maid brought in a tray. There was jam and crumpets and tea and strawberries.

"And what is this?" asked Mr. Bunny, poking at something buttery-looking in a little pot.

"That's clotted cream, sir," said the maid, and then padded out.

"Their cream *clots*?" said Mr. Bunny. "Hmmm. Don't like the sound of that. Blood clots. Blood is supposed to clot. That's how you get scabs. But Mr. Bunny doesn't care for clotty comestibles or scabby cream. It's against nature."

"Oh, Mr. Bunny, don't be a poo," said Mrs. Bunny, slathering clotted cream on a crumpet. "Everything probably clots here. It's probably just a very clotty country."

"Mrs. Bunny, you never told me how travel makes you rhapsodic. I don't believe I would have married you if I had known."

"Don't be silly, Mr. Bunny. My rhapsodies are one of my finest features. What kind of creature was that maid? She wasn't a bunny or a marmot. I can't seem to place the species."

"I know what she is. It's on the tip of my tongue," said Mr. Bunny. "There were some of them in *Alice in Wonderland*."

"Well, let me know when it comes to you, Mr. Bunny. My, this room has wonderful dimensions. It would be very spacious if it weren't for all these bushes they seem to be storing in it. Pots and pots of bushes."

"I prefer Canada and its custom of keeping the bushes outdoors. Have the last crumpet? No? Don't mind if I do."

He popped it into his mouth and swallowed.

"I was going to suggest we split it," said Mrs. Bunny.

"Too late," said Mr. Bunny, and sighed with satisfaction. "I like a good breakfast. It helps to kick my big bunny brains into gear. Big breakfast, big brains. Little breakfast, little brains."

"I prefer a light breakfast myself," said Mrs. Bunny.

Mr. Bunny just smiled. He did so like it when Mrs. Bunny made his point for him.

Mrs. Bunny caught his smile and was about to retort when there was another knock on the door and there stood Mrs. Treaclebunny.

"Come on then, get dressed and come downstairs," she said briskly. "You must meet my cousin, the Duchess of Bungleyhog."

"A *duchess*?" said Mrs. Bunny. "You didn't tell us you were related to a duchess."

"I do not like to toot my own horn," said Mrs. Treacle-bunny. "Watch yourselves around her, I warn you, because she's very prickly."

Mrs. Treaclebunny closed the door and the Bunnys swiftly got out of their pajamas and into respectable meeting-a-duchess clothes.

"Of course she'll be prickly," said Mrs. Bunny. "So much of the aristocracy is. When I am made queen, I plan to be very prickly indeed. I plan to prickle all over the place."

"I'm sure you will," said Mr. Bunny as they came down the stairs. There stood Mrs. Treaclebunny speaking to a very odd-looking animal in a riding habit.

"Who do you suppose that can be?" asked Mrs. Bunny.

"Ah," said Mrs. Treaclebunny. "Mr. and Mrs. Bunny, may I present my cousin, the Duchess of Bungleyhog."

"How do you do. Is it Miss or Mrs. Bungleyhog?" asked Mr. Bunny.

Mrs. Bunny thought again how fortunate it was that she and Mr. Bunny had become fluent in English so they could now join in the duchessy conversation.

Mr. Bunny held out his hand in his best Canadian manner. "Or Ms.?"

"It's Duchess Bungleyhog," said the duchess.

"I like to call her Bungs. Of course, I can do that because I am related," said Mrs. Treaclebunny.

"Yes, dear, but I do wish you'd stop announcing that in public," said the duchess. "After all, no one need really know we're related. And for heaven's sakes, try to look more like a hedgehog. It was bad enough when it was just you and Mr. Treaclebunny, God rest his poor disintegrating fur, but now that you're bringing all your rabbit cohorts to visit"—heavy sigh—"I really think the best thing is to try to disguise you all. You will never look like the *best* of hedgehogs, but you could try to look a *little* more hedgy and a lot more hoggy. Violet, bring me my extra quills."

"That's what they are!" Mr. Bunny whispered excitedly to Mrs. Bunny. "They're hedgehogs!"

"Shhh," said Mrs. Bunny.

"You said to tell you when it came to me!"

"It didn't *come* to you. She *told* you she was a hedgehog. Now shh."

"You shh."

"Both of you shh!" said Mrs. Treaclebunny.

The duchess's maid, Violet, scooted out of the room and was back a short time later with the duchess's makeup kit. Inside was a large bag of extra quills that the duchess put on when she was going to a particularly fancy event. With hedge-hogs, the more quills, the better. She and Violet stuck them into the bunnies' fur with Krazy Glue. When they were finished the bunnies didn't look so much like hedgehogs as like rabbits with quills stuck in them, but the duchess seemed satisfied.

"Ouch," said Mr. Bunny when he bumped against the wall and accidentally stuck himself.

"You look enchanting," said the duchess charitably. "Not up to hedgehog snuff, of course, but *much* better than before. You can certainly pass. I can bring you to dinners and teas. If anyone suggests you look like rabbits I will say, 'But look at the quills.' It will work, I think, yes, it will work."

"OW!" said Mr. Bunny, sticking himself again accidentally and jumping into the air in a most unhedgehoglike manner. "The quills have got to go. And how the heck can you be Mrs. Treaclebunny's cousin? You're a hedgehog and she's a rabbit. It doesn't make sense."

Mrs. Bunny put her hands in front of her face in agony. Could he never control himself? Why must he always ask the questions that everyone else knew better than to ask? And why did he never mind the embarrassment this caused Mrs. Bunny?

"So many want to be hedgehogs, but so few are," said the duchess. "Every so often we hedgehogs have a misalliance in the family because of this. There is so much social climbing. *Particularly* among rabbits. Hedgehogs never need social-climb because we are at the top. But other animals—they all want to be hedgehogs."

"*I* don't," said Mr. Bunny.

"HUSH," said Mrs. Bunny, pulling his tail.

"We hedgehogs are used to it. But when such a misalliance happens in the family, we feel it is best for all concerned to *hide* it."

"I don't see how you figure you're better than rabbits," said Mr. Bunny, beginning to shift from foot to foot truculently.

Uh-oh, thought Mrs. Bunny, pulling at her fur. Couldn't Mr. Bunny understand that you just don't talk to a duchess that way? He was going to screw up all her chances of being queen if he didn't put a lid on it. With social climbing it was *essential* to know how to grovel.

"*How* are we better than you? We are better than you, you ridiculous lapin, because we can do *this*." The duchess curled herself into a ball and rolled forward, accidentally bumping into Mrs. Bunny.

"OW," said Mrs. Bunny.

"Well, I could go around doing somersaults and sticking people with forks; I don't see that it would make me superior," said Mr. Bunny.

"Shut up," said Mrs. Bunny sotto voce.

"I don't get that at all," said Mr. Bunny.

"Shut up, shut up, shut up," muttered Mrs. Bunny into Mr. Bunny's ear while pretending to fix his collar.

But the Duchess of Bungleyhog was paying no attention. She seldom did to rabbits.

"Now I'm off to the hunt. Cheerio. Do enjoy your stay. I'll arrange some dinners and teas with your betters and we'll see if we can't get you at least one rung up the social ladder. Perhaps we can get you into viscountdom or maybe earldom."

"OOOOOO!" trilled Mrs. Bunny shrilly. "Did you hear that, Mr. Bunny, you could be pronounced an earl."

"I could be pronounced a fried egg too, Mrs. Bunny. Try not to shriek in my ear every time you hear a title. I don't wish to be a member of the aristocracy, but if I must, I prefer not to be a deaf member."

"Try not to annoy my staff and don't engage in any obvious rabbit behavior," said the duchess, who hadn't listened to a word anyone but she herself had said, as was her habit. "Remember, you're hedgehogs now."

Then she swept out.

"I've had enough of this nonsense," said Mr. Bunny. "What does she take me for?" He started to pull out his quills.

"No, no!" said Mrs. Bunny. "Please, Mr. Bunny. For just a while longer. It's a means to an end. It's a shortcut to being queen. And as soon as I'm queen, we can go home."

"Humph," said Mr. Bunny again, but he stopped pulling out quills. He was certainly ready to go home. He'd had quite enough of the whole traveling business. He wanted his own hutch and comestibles that didn't clot. "Coming all the way across the ocean to room with bushes!"

"Those are not ordinary bushes, Mr. Bunny. Those are hedgerows," said Mrs. Treaclebunny. "England used to have miles and miles of hedgerows until the duchess's ancestors decided to collect them. Her family has been digging them up and bringing them to the castle for a century now. The British keep complaining that miles of hedgerows have disappeared over the years but no one knows where they've gone. Someone suggested that flying saucers took them while making the crop circles."

"Flying saucers!" snorted Mr. Bunny. "The fantasy worlds some people live in!"

"Anyhow, Mrs. Bunny," said Mrs. Treaclebunny. "I told you Bungs would help us up the social ladder. In no time at all we shall be queens. I haven't told her that's the ultimate goal yet, but she has oodles of brilliant connections. We can have tea and make our way up from duchesses to earlesses to princesses, and then in very little time queendom will be upon us."

"Oh! Oh!" said Mrs. Bunny, clasping her paws in rapture.

"Queendom will be upon *us*?" said Mr. Bunny. "I thought it was only Mrs. Bunny who wanted to be queen."

"The idea has grown on me," said Mrs. Treaclebunny. "I especially like the thought of ruling. When I was a young bunny, ruling the world was one of my career aspirations. But my family could only afford nursing school."

"But, Mrs. Treaclebunny," said Mrs. Bunny, "I really think there can be only *one* queen."

"Yes, exactly," said Mrs. Treaclebunny. "I will be queen and you can be the subqueen."

"Why do I have to be the subqueen?" asked Mrs. Bunny. "It was *my* idea."

"Because *my* cousin is the duchess," said Mrs. Treaclebunny, and that was the end of that. "Now, the duchess has gone on a hunt. We have a free day before the social climbing begins. What shall we do with our first day in England? Shall we explore the nearby village of Bellyflop?"

"Bellyflop!" said Mrs. Bunny, falling over in disbelief. "Are we that near to Bellyflop? But that's where Madeline is staying."

"Is it? That's an amazing coincidence," said Mrs. Treacle-bunny.

"The kind usually found only in books," agreed Mr. Bunny.

"Which is very convenient, as I shan't have to make it up when I come to write up our adventures in my new book," said Mrs. Bunny. She got out her writing book and scribbled:

> Note to self, amazing coincidence that the bunnies now practically next door to Madeline. Or perhaps—synchronicity?

"Not again!" said Mr. Bunny, who was reading over her shoulder. He tried to read the notes she took for her new books whenever possible. Now and then he forged a few in Mrs. Bunny's handwriting, hoping she would mistake them for her own.

*Mr. Bunny—the first super rabbit? Mind like a steel trap!* read one.

*Mr. Bunny—so funny ought to do stand-up!* read another.

*Mr. Bunny, so brilliant! Like staring at the sun!*

He had crossed this last out as perhaps too over-the-top. Writing was so difficult.

"I suppose we can agree to disagree," said Mrs. Bunny as they hopped across the moat. She was not going to argue with him very strenuously. It was enough that he hadn't pulled out his quills.

"Pffff," said Mr. Bunny. He wasn't going to argue with Mrs. Bunny. He just wanted to see her crowned and get home in time for the football season.

It was a short hop to the village. When the bunnies got there Madeline's family's sweet shoppe was easy to find. It had a large sign out front saying SWEET SHOPPE.

The shoppe was already open and behind the counter were Mildred, Flo, Madeline, Katherine and a little man the bunnies didn't recognize. Mildred and Flo and the man were in such a loud conversation that no one even heard the shoppe bell tinkle as the rabbits entered.

"I'm terribly sorry. I shall have my secretary fired at once, of course. Dear, dear, to think you crossed the Atlantic under such a misapprehension," said the little man with a worried expression.

"Not to mention circumnavigating the North and South American continents," said Flo. "But hey, man, it's not the destination, it's the journey."

"Yes, ahem, as I was saying, to think you came all this way because my secretary made a typo."

"So," said Mildred, "you're saying that the sweet shoppe *didn't* clear a hundred thousand pounds in the month of August alone, as we read in your letter?"

"Ahem, not quite."

"So it made only ten thousand pounds?"

"No, no."

"Well, thank heavens for that, because ten thousand pounds isn't enough for Zanky's thirty acres," said Mildred. "So! What did it clear?"

"Well, under the circumstances, I'm not sure you want to know," said the man.

"Just tell us!" yelled Mildred.

"One thousand pounds," said the man in a small voice.

"WHAT!" said Mildred.

"Of course, that's about sixteen hundred of your Canadian dollars. Give or take a few dollars. That's a little better. Although"—he paused and cleared his throat and finished in a smaller voice—"not really."

"One thousand pounds? That's all the shop made in August? One thousand pounds? We'd have to stay here a couple of *years* to make enough to buy Zanky's acreage."

"Yeah, and we've got to be on the cruise ship for our return gig," said Flo. "We can't stay two years, man."

"We're in a recession. So many out of work, you see. So much unemployment. There just hasn't been money for extras in so many households. And I'm afraid sweets are, ahem, rather an extra. Now I must get back to my office. Sorry for the confusion. And who knows, perhaps you can find a way to turn a better profit in August. Don't you have that Yankee ingenuity we hear so much about?"

"Yankees are American," said Katherine.

"We're Canadians," said Madeline. When *would* people learn to tell the difference?

"Right. Still, I hope you enjoy your stay."

When the man left, Mildred pulled up a chair and sat down heavily. "Well, that's that," she said. "We may as well just turn around and go home."

"Hey, synchronicity. I'm the Dalai Lama of sugar, remember? I'm bringing sugar to the people. Who cares if we make any money?"

"Flo, the whole *point* of coming here was to make money so that we could buy Zanky's thirty acres," said Mildred wearily.

"The whole point of buying Zanky's thirty acres was to have money for my college education," Madeline whispered to Katherine.

"We don't know what the point of anything is," said Flo. "It's in the stars, man."

"Your college education?" said Mildred, who had overheard Madeline.

"Well, if you sold your vegetables at the market you would make money. And you never care about money, so I thought I could use it for college," said Madeline.

"Oh man, more school?" said Flo. "That's, like, perverse."

"But could I have it?" asked Madeline. "Just hypothetically?"

"College? I thought you wanted to be a silversmith. College is just nonse—" began Mildred, when the bell on the door tinkled and in strode a woman. She was dressed all in tweeds with her hair in an updo and wearing a pair of dark glasses. She looked rich and busy and very important and very British, but when she spoke she had an American accent.

"How do you do? The Twickenham Twill school is having a charity fete, and we are asking local shoppe owners to set up booths selling their wares and donate the . . . HARRY?" She pushed up her sunglasses and stared. "And under all that dyed blond hair, my gracious, can it be? Is it you, Denise?"

Mildred blushed. "I just had my hair dyed for . . . an . . . event. It's usually still brown. But can it be you? Starlight Heavens from the Haight?"

"I prefer to be called Lady Henderson now," said Starlight Heavens. "Or Jean. I married a lord. I live on the outside of this extremely amusing little British village. My husband inherited the family estate. We live in a *manor* house." She could not help preening when she said this.

"Ooo!" said Mrs. Bunny.

"Shh," said Mr. Bunny. So far no one had noticed them hiding behind a large candy carton in the corner.

"Wow," said Flo. "Cool."

"Are you still teaching yoga? And doing those macramé wall hangings?" asked Mildred, who kept touching her hair self-consciously and looking uncomfortable.

Lady Henderson gave a tinkling little laugh. "Oh no. I'm very busy running the *manor* house."

"You gotta paint and mow the lawn and stuff, I guess. And put out mousetraps. Old houses," said Flo, nodding sympathetically.

Lady Henderson laughed again. "No, Harry, we have servants for that. But that's precisely what I mean. I have so *many* servants to manage. And then there are the charity fetes for the children's school. They go to public school, of course."

"We go to public school," said Katherine from behind the counter.

Lady Henderson hadn't noticed the girls. Now she peered over the counter at them. "Yours, I suppose?" she asked Mildred, taking a step back as if the girls perhaps needed delousing.

"*Madeline* is our daughter," said Mildred. "This is Katherine. She's spending the summer with us. We aren't Harry and Denise anymore. We prefer to be called Flo and Mildred now."

"On the lam?" said Lady Henderson. "Anyhow, little girl, in England public school is what you would call private school. You do not go to public school in our sense of the word."

"How does *she* know?" muttered Katherine to Madeline when Lady Henderson had turned back to Mildred.

"I see you've bought this old white elephant. I hope you didn't do it for the money. No one shops here. No one of importance. We all get our sweets from London. In fact, I don't know anyone who patronizes the local shoppes. Except, of course, those who are not our type. Oh, I forgot . . . perhaps they're *your* type."

"Well, now that you're here, want to buy something? We have dolly mix and Gin Gins and Gray's Herbal Tablets," said Flo, reading names off boxes and canisters.

Lady Henderson took another step back.

"Good gracious, I never buy such junk for little Ermintrude and Alfred. They get their chocolates from the Queen's chocolatiers. After all, we have to prepare them for their places in society. They were born at the Queen's hospital, of course, with the Queen's own obstetrician on hand. And then they went to Sloane Street Prep Preschool to get into Her Ladyship's

Kindergarten so that they could proceed to Twickenham Twill Elementary and on to Oxford eventually." This took all of Lady Henderson's breath and she stood panting.

"All that school," said Flo sadly, shaking his head.

"Well, we don't want them to grow up to be *shoppe owners*," said Lady Henderson. "Not when their father once had dinner with the queen."

"Dinner with the QUEEN?" cried Mrs. Bunny.

At that, Flo turned his head and spied the bunnies behind the carton. He whispered to Mildred, "Man, remember when the kidnappers drugged us and we hallucinated rabbits? Well, it's happening again."

"Shut up," said Mildred.

"Who cried out 'Dinner with the QUEEN?'" demanded Lady Henderson, looking around.

Mildred kicked another carton in front of the bunnies. She was pretty sure the rabbits didn't exist, but then why did Lady Henderson hear them? Mildred didn't have time to think about it now—she must salvage the situation. She squealed, "*Who* shrieked 'Dinner with the QUEEN?' That was me."

"No, it wasn't," said Lady Henderson.

"Of course it was. Unless you're hallucinating talking rabbits or something," laughed Mildred.

"Our sort never hallucinates," said Lady Henderson, sniffing.

"Anyway," said Mildred, quickly changing the subject, "Madeline plans to go to *Harvard* when she graduates. I plan to buy a large organic vegetable farm with the money we make on the shoppe this summer. And that, of course, will more than finance Harvard."

"What? Make money on *this* shoppe?"

"Yes," said Mildred stubbornly.

"But this shoppe doesn't *make* money, dear," said Lady Henderson, laughing.

"It will. We have plans," said Mildred.

"That's adorable. You know," said Lady Henderson, turning to Madeline, "Harvard is difficult to get into. It's not like one of your little provincial universities. You *are* lucky to be in Canada. It's so easy to get into schools there. I was going to ask you to have a booth at our fete and donate the proceeds but, of course, I can see now you need *every nickel.* Too bad, because it's quite a large affair. We invite the locals from six counties, so it would be a very good advertisement for you. Lots of your sort shopping and playing games. You wouldn't feel too outclassed."

"We'll be at your charity fete," said Mildred through gritted teeth.

"Yeah, man, we, like, always like to give back," said Flo. "And meeting you here is, like, more synchronicity."

Mildred kicked him.

"Well, toodle-oo," said Lady Henderson, and she swept out.

"Toodle-doodle-poodle-oo to you," said Mildred. Her arms were crossed and she was beginning to twitch.

Madeline was staring at her mother, who had always taught her that everyone was equal and money was the root of all evil. This was not Hornby Island Mildred or even Cruising Mildred. This was some strange new Mildred whom Madeline had never seen before. Off her own turf, Mildred seemed to be like a rudderless ship that floundered on the open sea. I wanted her to be different, thought Madeline, but not like this and not like Cruising Mildred. When she thought about it, she realized she had never had a concrete idea of the way she wanted Mildred to be. Only the ways she didn't want her to be.

Mildred's live-and-let-live ways seemed to have disintegrated in the presence of Lady Henderson. Madeline looked worriedly at her mother's twitching face.

"That's it. We're making this shoppe pay if it's the last thing we do!" said Mildred.

"Hey, man, you're not doing this just to spite Lady Henderson, are you?" asked Flo.

"Yes, Flo, I am. This is spite profit."

"Wow," said Flo. "But, like, how?"

"I . . . I . . . ," said Mildred, appearing to deflate again. "I'm afraid I haven't the least idea."

Madeline's parents seemed to have forgotten the bunnies hidden in the corner, but she hadn't. They had turned up, as they always seemed to, just when she needed them. She had faith in Mr. Bunny. Mr. Bunny was always full of ideas. They weren't always the *best* ideas, but he had them one after another. He would surely save the day.

## ◄THE ASPARAGUS CONTRETEMPS►

It was, of course, a joyous reunion between the Bunnys and Madeline and Katherine. They ran outside the shoppe so that the Bunnys could tell them how they had ended up in Belly-flop.

"I can't believe that *just* as I get Mildred to agree to give me her vegetable money for a college fund, we can't afford to buy the land to grow the vegetables!" said Madeline.

"I can't believe the candy shoppe doesn't make money. Who doesn't like candy?" said Mrs. Bunny. "Mr. Bunny is very fond of black licorice."

"And jelly beans!" said Mr. Bunny.

"We'll just have to find a way," said Mrs. Bunny. "That must be our first priority in England, Mr. Bunny."

"What about your social climbing?" asked Mr. Bunny.

"The female of the species is an adept multitasker," said Mrs. Bunny. "We task. We task all over the place."

"Mr. Bunny, I thought maybe you'd have one of your good ideas," said Madeline.

"Ah!" said Mr. Bunny, putting his hands behind him and pacing back and forth. "Indeed. Indeedy, deedy do. Mr. Bunny is a wealth of ideas."

"Try for one," said Mrs. Treaclebunny sourly. "And don't forget we need to get back to the castle in time for lunch. The duchess has invited an assortment of the titled gentry."

"Oh, Mr. Bunny!" said Mrs. Bunny. "The full assortment!"

"Mrs. Bunny, calm yourself. This is no time to drool over dukes. We're busy saving the day," said Mr. Bunny.

"I can't think why no one has asked *me* what to do," said Mrs. Treaclebunny. "I'm the only one here with any actual business experience. Mr. Bunny was on the carrot marketing board and Mrs. Bunny made lint art—"

"Isn't the carrot marketing board a business?" interrupted Katherine.

"To rabbits," said Mrs. Treaclebunny, "anything involving carrots is practically a religion. Now, Mr. Treaclebunny, God rest his poor dead festering feet, and I ran a *real* business. We had a rubber factory. I can give you important advice. I will dole it out in dribs and drabs so as not to overwhelm your brains. Here is the first drib: I think we must get the lay of the land. We must check out the other shoppes in town and see who is successful and why. I may know the ins and outs of business in Canada, but this is England. Their ins are different."

"And their outs," said Mrs. Bunny, nodding.

"No," said Mrs. Treaclebunny. "Their outs are very much the same."

Madeline dashed into the shoppe to tell Mildred and Flo that she and Katherine were going exploring. They just nodded glumly and waved her away. No one had come into the shoppe except Lady Henderson, and they were anticipating a long, dull, profitless day.

Then the bunnies and the girls tromped up and down the main street of Bellyflop. There was a bookstore and a tailor. There was a small grocery and a chemist. Everyone seemed to be doing a thriving business. Even the tailor.

"I find this most odd," said Mrs. Treaclebunny. "Does everyone need tailoring but no one needs candy?"

"Hmmm," said Mr. Bunny. "I must put on my thinking cap."

He looked as if he were about to do it that very second, so Mrs. Treaclebunny looked at her watch and yelled, "LUNCH!" and began hopping toward the castle.

"She's rather abrupt, isn't she?" said Katherine.

"You don't know the half of it," said Mr. Bunny, and they hopped after her to the castle.

Once inside the castle, they found that the whole hunting party had assembled with cocktails. The duchess took one look at Madeline and Katherine and stood up on her chair to cry, "HUMANS!" in the exact way some people react to mice.

All conversation stopped.

"They're our pets," said Mrs. Bunny, clearing her throat.

"Give them bowls in the kitchen, then. Don't bring them in *here,*" said the duchess.

"I'm so sorry," said Mrs. Bunny to the girls as she led them into the kitchen and the cook set a couple of bowls of chopped vegetables on the floor for them.

"That's all right," said Madeline. "Just do what you have to do to be queen. We understand."

"Don't worry, I'll keep an eye on your pets," said the cook. "They're kind of shaggy. When's the last time they were groomed?"

"How dare you!" said Katherine.

"Sit!" said the cook.

The girls sat.

Mrs. Bunny looked vexed, but of course, she could say nothing. Instead she slunk back into the dining room and found her place card. She was seated between an earl hedgehog and a duke hedgehog. They both slurped their soup.

"So," said the earl. "Visiting, I hear. And had a hot year wherever you're from, judging by your coat."

"What?" said Mrs. Bunny, who was rattled by all the titles and was busily trying to memorize who was who, in order to figure out where to begin her social climbing.

"Lack of quills. Been shedding a bit too, I see," said the earl. "And growing an awful lot of *fur*." He shuddered.

"OH!" said Mrs. Bunny, turning red.

"That's a very peculiar name you have too," said a viscountess, reading Mrs. Bunny's place card. "With no *hog* at the end. Are you sure it isn't Bunnyhog and Treaclebunnyhog?"

"Uh, uh, uh," stammered Mrs. Bunny, blushing.

"They're from *Canada*!" said Duchess Bungleyhog.

Everybody nodded. That explained *everything*.

"Lot of beavers there," said the viceroy, turning to the vicereine.

"Well, they can't help *that*," said the marchioness from across the table. She was one of the more liberal hedgehogs.

"I suppose the hedgehogs in Canada have evolved to have such long ears as yours so as to be found when buried under snow!" said the earl with sudden inspiration. He was quite pleased with himself. It had been twelve years since he'd had an original thought.

"Tell me, how fares the Canadian muskeg?" asked the marquis, turning to Mr. Bunny.

"Musky. Oooo, what's this I see?" said Mr. Bunny as the footman approached him with a platter. "Fish sticks!"

When he could not get as many as he liked with the serving fork, he tipped the platter that the footman was holding and poured a pile onto his plate. "Yum, yum. Lightened your load, my good man!"

Mrs. Bunny shredded the napkin in her lap. Mr. Bunny was going to become all jokey with the servants. Mrs. Bunny could never decide which was more embarrassing, Mr. Bunny in his jocular moods or Mr. Bunny in his cantankerous moods. They both bore watching.

"I suppose that explains the fur," whispered the margrave. "Intermarriage with beavers."

"Nonsense, Stinky," boomed Duchess Bungleyhog, who had overheard. "They're from the less-quilled side of the family. From the hedgehog genus *Nonpricklum*. They're born practically quill-less."

There was a gasp about the table and then everyone looked politely away.

"How unfortunate," said the vicereine to Mr. Bunny. "I shall tell no one."

"Tell anyone you want," said Mr. Bunny, shrugging. "Just pass the mashed potatoes."

Mrs. Bunny tried to kick Mr. Bunny under the table but only managed to kick some heavily quilled leg. Whoever it was didn't seem to feel it, but Mrs. Bunny got a quill stuck in her toe. It would make wearing high heels nearly impossible for weeks to come.

"Oh dear, oh dear, Your Earldom," said Mrs. Bunny, talking rapidly to cover up for Mr. Bunny's swiftly mounting faux pas. The earl turned to her, but this was where Mrs. Bunny came a cropper. She had nothing to say. Whatever did you talk to an earl about? She doubted he'd be interested in her lint art. Or her used-dental-floss knitting.

"Oh my, have you seen the new, er, hat styles this season?" she finally inquired.

"No," said the earl.

That might have ended it, but he continued to stare at her with soup dribbling down his chin.

Mrs. Bunny looked toward Mr. Bunny beseechingly. She could always count on him to rescue her when she ran out of conversation. Mr. Bunny needed very little encouragement to run off at the mouth. Then she decided this was such a good observation that she got out her writing notebook and wrote:

*Mr. Bunny needed little encouragement to engage in displays of verbal diarrhea.*

She was chuckling over her way with words when the earl startled her by booming, "What are you doing?"

"I am taking notes. I'm a writer," said Mrs. Bunny, trying to look modest.

"Good God, you don't WORK, do you?" asked the earl.

Mrs. Bunny looked beseechingly at Mr. Bunny again, but he had built up a fierce appetite that morning with all the hopping back and forth across moats and he had piled his plate high with mashed potatoes, turnip greens and boiled mashed asparagus and was now attempting to balance a mound of beets upon his already overloaded plate. It was a task of some architectural difficulty and required all his concentration.

"My, these mashed asparagus are delicious," said Mrs. Bunny in desperation, spooning up a heaping mound and cramming them into her mouth. "I shall have to ask the duchess for her recipe." Unfortunately, in her haste she had taken too large a mouthful of their mashed greeny goodness. She coughed expulsively and some of it spurted out, attaching in sticky mounds to the earl's shirt and quilly chest.

"OH DRAT!" said Mrs. Bunny.

Now everyone at the table except the earl was staring at her. He was staring at his shirt.

There was a long ominous silence.

"Oh dear, is that my mashed asparagus on your shirtfront?" Mrs. Bunny finally asked. Then, because everyone continued to stare silently and something else seemed to be required of her, she spooned up a forkful from between two of his buttons and said, "YUM!"

There was another moment of silence, during which even Mr. Bunny stared at her quizzically as if he couldn't quite place from which roadside ditch or bog he had found her. Then conversation resumed around the table, and the earl turned to his other tablemate and attempted no more polite conversation with Mrs. Bunny.

"Oh dear," said Mrs. Bunny again. Now no one was talking to her and it was very lonely. Maybe Mr. Bunny is right, she thought, maybe I should engage less in haberdashery chitchat and more in current affairs. I will read the *Bunny Post* first thing tomorrow. She turned with sudden inspiration to the earless, who sat on her other side. "Have you ever noticed how *earless,*

the feminine form of *earl,* if looked at differently is not *earl-ess* but *ear-less?*"

The earless gave her a long flat look and began a conversation with the viscount.

Mrs. Bunny blushed and blushed. I *am* banal, she said to herself. Very, *very* banal.

"What did you say *your* title was?" asked the duke.

"Mrs.," squeaked Mrs. Bunny.

"I see," said the duke. "Canada, eh? Are you friends with the Bronfman hedgehogs? The Mulroney hedgehogs? Any of that crowd?"

"Er," said Mrs. Bunny. "We are certainly in a crowd. You know, the, uh, lots-of-important-types crowd."

"What brings you to these parts? I thought it was prime hedgehog season in Canada. Everyone finally out of hibernation. You *do* hibernate, don't you?"

"Oh, we hiber, we don't always nate," said Mrs. Bunny, a bundle of fluster.

"What is it you want to do here?" asked the earless. "Our hedges are all spoken for, you know."

"I say, is that what you Canadian hedgehogs are doing here? Come to England to steal our hedges because you've run out of your own? Explain to us, please, what your country is besides a boggy beaver backwater." And thus, having attained international alliterative excellence, the duke sat back in his chair, as did everyone else, and stared at her silently. Mrs. Bunny was getting very tired of being stared at. They were politely awaiting her answer. All except Mr. Bunny. He was making good headway in his attack on the victuals. By consistent and steady forking up, he had almost made his way through the mashed asparagus and was about to move on to the potatoes. He stared at his plate with fixed attention.

Mrs. Bunny didn't answer. In fact, she thought she might be having a heart attack. It was so hard to tell under all that fur. She tried to take her pulse but a new outcry arose from down the table.

"Of course, the Canadians want our carefully stolen hedgerows!" cried the czarina.

"First it's the hedges, then it's our Tetley tea."

"Yes, that's what you want, isn't it?"

"Is it the Tetley tea or the hedgerows? You're here to steal the best of Britain and claim it as your own!"

"It's our clotted cream!"

"It's not your clotted cream," muttered Mr. Bunny to himself through a mouthful of mashed asparagus. "I can guarantee that."

"That's what you want indeed!"

"Or is it? Tell us! Tell us right now what it is you want!"

Poor Mrs. Bunny. Suddenly she felt herself in a fun-house hall of mirrors, with all the distorted faces crying, "TELL US!" It was doing her heart attack no good at all.

She pulled at her ears and bellowed, "I JUST WANT TO BE QUEEN!"

There was silence at the table.

Then the laughter began.

# A SURPRISE FOR MRS. BUNNY

"I don't suppose," said the Duchess of Bungleyhog to the three bunnies as she showed them out after lunch, "we can call your first attempt at social climbing a great success."

"I think perhaps spitting mounds of asparagus onto others is better saved for the family board," said Mr. Bunny mildly to Mrs. Bunny while nonchalantly pulling a toothpick from the ever-ready supply in his pocket and using it assiduously.

Mrs. Bunny just stared at him tiredly. None of the things she could think of to say were ladylike.

"We *may* be able to patch things up," said the duchess. "First of all, before making any more social forays, I suggest you buy a title. Here is a list of available ones. They are only forty-nine ninety-nine. Plus shipping and handling."

The bunnies sat down, and after long perusing, Mr. Bunny said there was nothing he would like to be so much as Mr. Bunny so you could count him right out.

"What about pharaoh?" said Mrs. Bunny enticingly.

"I decline all titles," said Mr. Bunny. "The whole thing is a sham. A sham and a scam."

"How about czar?" asked Mrs. Bunny, wringing her paws. "Wouldn't that be fun? You could buy one of those big furry Russian hats."

"It's always about the hats with you, isn't it?" said Mr. Bunny.

"But you can't come to any more social-climbing events with us unless you have a title," said Mrs. Bunny.

"Suits me fine," said Mr. Bunny, and he refused to even look at the list of titles after that.

"Oh, never mind him, every party has a pooper," said Mrs. Treaclebunny, who was reading the list. "Oooo! What's this? *Yang di-Pertuan Agong.* It says it's Malaysian for 'heavenly supreme lord.' That's the ticket. You notice the *supreme,* Mrs. Bunny? That means you won't be able to find a title to top mine."

"That's just like her," Mr. Bunny whispered in Mrs. Bunny's ear. "Hogging supreme lorddom for herself." And then this suddenly struck him as funny. A sound erupted from him.

At first he did not recognize what it was. It was unlike any of the usual eruptions he was known to have.

"Mr. Bunny, was that a giggle?" asked Mrs. Treaclebunny.

"No! No! No, indeed," said Mr. Bunny. "It was a burp."

"It didn't sound like a burp."

"It was a British burp."

"Why are you burping in British?" asked Mrs. Treaclebunny.

"Why wouldn't I?" asked Mr. Bunny, pleased he had, as usual, come up with such a clever rejoinder that it left Mrs. Treaclebunny without a reply. But privately he was thinking, This is no good. I am spending too much time in female company. The next thing you know I will be wanting to watch television shows about picking wedding dresses. I must do something about this, and fast.

"You can't be a heavenly supreme lord, Mrs. Treaclebunny, how many times do I have to tell you that?" said the duchess witheringly. "You have to have a female title. Besides, what is the good of having a title no one can pronounce? Also, I can't say for sure, but I think you might be expected to go about answering people's prayers. Frankly, I don't think you have it in you. Start small, that's my advice."

"Small schmall. If I'm going to spend forty-nine ninety-nine I want to be something supreme. I like to get my money's worth," retorted Mrs. Treaclebunny, who was tired of being pushed around by her quilled relatives. She was reading the list of titles with a dissatisfied air. It was hard to go from heavenly supreme lord to the more land-based honors. "Well, I suppose I could start as a baroness. I notice there weren't any at lunch. I'd stand out."

"You already stand out, thanks to the reckless way you treat your quills. I sent you all out this morning charmingly bequilled and now look at you," said the duchess.

It was true, the quills had a tendency to get caught on things, ripping the fur in little patches. The bunnies stared at each other in dismay.

"We look like we're molting," said Mrs. Bunny dismally. "Wait a second—if I can buy the title of baroness, why don't I just buy the title of queen and be done with it?"

"The title of queen is not for sale. Because unlike the other titles, there can only be one," said the duchess. "I wouldn't go for queen anyway. One must be first in battle, last at the feed trough. I don't see the point myself."

"Well, maybe one can buy a lower title and work one's way up!" said Mrs. Bunny, beginning to get frenzied. "You see, Mr. Bunny, you must take a title or you will have nothing to work from."

"I am Mr. Bunny," said Mr. Bunny firmly. "For so I am called. I have no desire to be queen."

"Well, of course *you* would be *king*. You know how good you are at these things, Mr. Bunny. You are sure to become king before I work my way up to be queen. And if you're king, then I'm *automatically* queen. That's where we should have started to begin with. Figure out how to become king immediately, Mr. Bunny! Do it! Do it! Do it!" said Mrs. Bunny, hopping up and down hysterically.

"Let us go find Madeline and Katherine," said Mr. Bunny patiently in the gentle tone he used when he was on the verge of having Mrs. Bunny committed. "Have you forgotten that we were supposed to be using our big bunny brains to solve the sweet shoppe dilemma, aka the college fund dilemma?"

"That's what it is to be a rabbit, I suppose," said the duchess. "Always a dilemma. Hedgehogs have no dilemmas. No problems, no dilemmas, many hedges. It's in Latin on our family crest. Well, good luck to you. I'm back to the hunt. You can leave a check for the full amount of your titles on the coffee table. Forty-nine ninety-nine a title, plus two hundred eighty-seven. Finder's fee to me."

"Nice little racket you have going," said Mr. Bunny, getting out his checkbook. "That's another forty-nine ninety-nine, plus shipping and handling and finder's fee, I'll never see again."

"Don't forget to include the cost of my title," said Mrs.

Treaclebunny. "You don't think I'm paying for my own. After all, it's my cousin's castle you're staying at."

Mr. Bunny lowered his eyebrows menacingly, but he wrote out the check for both.

Afterward he and Mrs. Treaclebunny hopped toward the kitchen to find the girls. Mrs. Bunny went back to the coffee table and filled out a form. That was just like Mr. Bunny, refusing to become king just when she needed him crowned most. Well, if that was his attitude, he didn't deserve to find out what title he was going to have. I think he'd make a splendid pharaoh, she said to herself. Then she wondered for a second if he could be an admiral. Was that a title or a rank? She pictured a white uniform and one of those fetching naval hats and she might have drooled just a bit on the carpet. But she could not find admiral on the list, so, she said to herself, pharaoh it must be. And, after all, they wore those toga things, didn't they? Mr. Bunny did have such nice legs. She got her checkbook out of her purse, made out another check and hopped swiftly off to join the rest.

When the bunnies joined the girls in the kitchen, Madeline said they had had a reasonable time with Cook.

"She tried to be kind," said Katherine. She looked at Madeline and they giggled. Mr. Bunny, to his consternation, found himself joining them. He tried to cover it with a large and ugly belch. The women stared at him with concern.

"Men make such *peculiar* noises," said Mrs. Treaclebunny.

"Yar, that we do!" said Mr. Bunny, dropping his voice to a baritone and for some reason taking on the locution of a pirate. Good, he thought, good. "Well, girls, did you eat?"

"Cook opened a can of Spam for us," said Katherine. "She said she was keeping it for just such an occasion."

"We managed to throw it out without her seeing," said Madeline.

"We didn't want to hurt her feelings."

"That's too bad about the Spam," said Mr. Bunny. "Mrs. Bunny had a contretemps herself with some mashed asparagus—"

"What shall we do with our afternoon?" interrupted Mrs. Bunny hastily.

"There are so many problems to be solved," said Mr. Bunny. "The sweet shoppe dilemma. The queen problem. Both will need concentrated solitude and hard thinking, the type of which you have never experienced, Mrs. Bunny. I must put on my great thinking cap and go to work alone on these things."

"Very well, dear," said Mrs. Bunny. "The girls and I will do some postcard and souvenir shopping in Bellyflop."

"Yippee!" said Mr. Bunny, clapping his paws. "I mean,

YAR." He shook himself. Something must be done. He must find a way to spend more time with male bunnies. He hopped upstairs to take a nap, shaking his head vexedly.

Mrs. Bunny, Mrs. Treaclebunny and the girls headed off and had a lovely time in the chemist. They examined all the different British products, looked about for the perfect snow globe and bought three postcards each, even though Madeline had no one to send them to. Then Katherine said she'd like to go back to the sweet shoppe to write her postcards and affix the stamps. She was anxious that her family know she was happily ensconced in Bellyflop. Mrs. Treaclebunny wanted to go in search of some fur cream and Mrs. Bunny decided she'd explore the rest of the town alone.

Meanwhile, Mr. Bunny was looking for the best place to take an excellent nap. I will say this about castle owners, he said to himself. They do know how to provide proper napping conditions.

The castle had many great halls to choose from, all equipped with large fireplaces. All the fireplaces had large flat-screen TVs over them, indicating, Mr. Bunny thought with glee, that the Bungleyhogs were not quite so refined as they might think. Not that Mr. Bunny did not wholeheartedly approve of this arrangement. He had often asked for just such an arrangement himself. Mrs. Bunny could be quite the stick-in-the-mud when it came to massive entertainment units. The Bungleyhogs, on the other hand, had large reclining chairs by their fires with cup holders and remote controls in the armrests. Mr. Bunny had never heard of such a thing. When he found out the chairs also had heated shiatsu-massage units, he began to think those Bungleyhogs very smart hedgehogs indeed. He spent a good half hour just playing with all the settings. He had not the slightest intention of thinking about the sweet shoppe or the queen problem. No, he could happily settle down to watch soccer, as planned. It was not football, he said to himself, but it was something.

After a while he fell into a deep drooling sleep. But it was not restful. He dreamt that Mrs. Treaclebunny and Mrs. Bunny had taken up dress design and were using him as a dressmaker's dummy. He was dreaming of standing in pink frills, being poked with pins, when he awoke. He noticed that during his sleep he had somehow leaned on the remote device in his armrest and the TV was now blaring a Shakespearean play. It was being acted by the famous Stratford all-male bunny Shakespeare players. How well went the fluffy tail with doublet, thought Mr. Bunny admiringly. But even more he admired their manner of speech. He remembered reading a great deal of Shakespeare in college. He had loved it dearly. He used to watch it on the bunny educational channel. Then along came Mrs. Bunny with her stupid haberdashery programs. *What to Wear and Whatnot. Say No to Those Pooey Wedding Dresses.* Not to mention the endless cooking shows she seemed to favor. He found life was always more peaceful when he handed Mrs. Bunny the clicker.

But what he had been missing! There was nothing like British bunny acting. He himself would not have read those lines *quite* like that, but still. Ah, what he could have done as an actor had he had the time. The time? Good heavens, Mr. Bunny, he said to himself, what do you have *except* time right now? And the place? Stratford was but one town over! Let someone else worry about the sweet shoppe and becoming queen—he needed a break from female companionship. He needed the company of some spitting, cursing, backslapping men. And what could be more fortuitous than finding this company of all-male bunny players? Not a giggling female in the lot. It was off to the stage with him! When Mrs. Bunny had attained all her royal goals she could just fetch him!

It was but the work of a moment to find some nail-polish remover in the bathroom and dissolve the Krazy Glue. The quills pulled right out after that. His fur was a bit mussed, but what care he? He was going to be with men who didn't care what their fur looked like. He was going to be in costume and onstage. He wrote Mrs. Bunny a quick note and left it on their bed:

> Dear Mrs. Bunny (for so you are called),
>     I have been taken by a theatrical turn. As you know, it is like getting the flu, only with better enunciation. I will tell you about my adventures before the footlights when I return, whenever that is. I would tell you them as I went along if you would only CARRY A CELL PHONE. How many times must I point out...

And he managed to fill another piece of paper with cell-phone badgering alone. The cell-phone argument was of long standing. Mr. Bunny wanted one. Mrs. Bunny did not. Now she will be sorry, he thought. Then, grabbing a few odds and ends, he attached them to a stick hobo-style and hopped off into what he was sure would eventually be the dramatic sunset such a bold move deserved.

When actual sunset came his feet were quite sore and he wasn't yet at Stratford. He thought of telling Mrs. Bunny the exciting tale of *The Long Hop,* as he had decided to title it, but realized she would be bound to say "I told you so" in that most irritating way she had.

And then, thinking of Mrs. Bunny and having a great many more miles to hop, he began to get annoyed at her suggestion that he couldn't come up with a good chapter title. Too wordy? Too *wordy*? What was *The Long Hop* if not an excellent succinct title? Ha! He could come up with not only better titles but better chapters than she could. To prove his point, he began to write one in his head:

*Mr. and Mrs. Bunny were going for their daily hop in the forest. As usual, Mr. Bunny was saying interesting things, many of which started with "Didja ever notice . . ." As usual, Mrs. Bunny struggled in vain to keep up, hopping-wise and interesting-things-wise.*

*"You know," said Mr. Bunny, "this should be your next book, right here."*

*"Huh," replied Mrs. Bunny with a faraway look in her eyes (which were excellent because of the vast amount of carrots she daily consumed). She was half listening to Mr. Bunny's interesting things, half thinking of a recipe for Maui carrots and half thinking of whether her fluffy tail and floppy ears needed a dye job. (Mathematically inclined readers will notice that three thinking halves equal more than one whole brain, but that never occurred to Mrs. Bunny.)*

*"What did you do this morning?" asked Mr. Bunny.*

*"I got up, fluffed my tail and sort of cleaned the hutch." (Neatness-inclined readers will notice last night's carrot sushi pans still on the stove, but that never occurred to Mrs. Bunny.)*

*"That's a chapter right there!" shouted Mr. Bunny triumphantly.*

*"How's that a chapter?" a bemused Mrs. Bunny asked, thinking about a hop later that day to Dinners, her favorite store, which offered many rabbit comestibles at discount prices. She was also thinking about whether her next author photo should focus less on her big floppy feet. And she was also practicing her acceptance speech, should her first book win the NBA (National Bunny Award). YB (young bunny)–inclined readers will notice that there was no such prize, but that never occurred to Mrs. Bunny.*

*"It must be hard for a marmot to order pie in a restaurant," cleverly observed Mr. Bunny.*

*"Huh?" replied Mrs. Bunny. Her eyes had lost their faraway look and had become mean red slits. (She could still see excellently well. The carrot thing again.)*

*"Mr. Bunny?" she said, her voice rising, falling and rising again, before settling into a trill three octaves above middle C.*

*"Yes?" replied Mr. Bunny. "For so I am called."*

*"Can it, marmotbreath!" said Mrs. Bunny, thus blowing any shot at the nonexistent NBA. But that never occurred to Mrs. Bunny.*

\*   \*   \*

Mr. Bunny would show her how inserting these bits by him improved the manuscript. And then he would go on to correct the mistakes she had made in her last book. For instance, she always wrote, *"Yes? For so I am called,"* said Mr. Bunny. When the proper way of writing it was *"Yes?" said Mr. Bunny. "For so I am called."* It was all in the details, as he had tried to tell her. But she never did listen, he thought, shaking his head sadly— long bunny ears though she had.

Well, writing was a piece of cake. And thinking of cake, he wondered if Mrs. Bunny would ever bake him another carrot cake once she found out he had left to join the stage and also hijacked the franchise. It would be too bad to be cakeless. On the other hand, from there on in, he could afford to *buy* cake, because he felt sure that if *he* wrote the books, they'd finally see some merchandising. He quickly took out the new notebook he'd bought to keep track of their trip expenses and wrote the story down so he wouldn't forget it. He would show it to Mrs. Bunny later as proof that he should write the books and she could go back to making wedding dresses out of used dental floss or whatever was her current short-lived enthusiasm.

Mr. Bunny was getting very thirsty hopping. He envisioned himself soon having a nice cold beer with the guys, having introduced himself by boldly hopping in and saying, "To be or not to be!" and having them all roar, "You must join us, you talented thespian bunny, you." Perhaps they would not repeat "you" in that manner. It sounded a little female-bunny-like. The thing was, Mr. Bunny had been around female bunnies for so long he was beginning to lose the male patter. No matter. Soon, he and his new thespian bunny pals would be at a pub together drinking beer and belching without a single "excuse me." The fact that Mr. Bunny didn't really like beer never entered into it. He preferred a good Diet Coke with ice, unless it was from a fast-food establishment, where they tried to rob you of your fair share of Coke by filling the cup with ice. Then he ordered his Coke iceless just to spite them. Or he preferred a good creamy hot chocolate the way Mrs. Bunny made it, with the extra marshmallows. That, unlike beer, went so well with shortbread cookies. Mr. Bunny was a dunker. Still, it was best to practice manly belching. And so he went along the country roads, hop belch, hop belch, hop hop belch belch belch, hop.

And so on.


Meanwhile, Madeline and Katherine had returned to the sweet shoppe to write their postcards and see how sales were going. They were surprised to find the shoppe closed and much activity happening. Flo and Mildred were in the kitchen. The floor was covered with crates and crates of vegetables. There were garbage cans full of Jelly Tots and Gin Gins.

"What's all this?" asked Madeline. "Why have you thrown out all the candy?"

"Flo had another idea," said Mildred.

"You know how Khartoum is at the confluence of the Blue Nile and the White Nile?" said Flo.

Madeline and Katherine nodded. They didn't, but with Flo this was expedient.

"It's confluence, man, it's all confluence. That's what creates synchronicity. All the clues point to it. And what's the confluence of your mother and myself?"

"Madeline?" asked Katherine.

"Heavy," said Flo. "But what I meant was the confluence between the Dalai Lama of sugar and the Mother Teresa of vegetables. *Vegetable candy!*"

Madeline looked dubious. "What *kind* of vegetable candy?"

"Chocolate-covered carrots. Sugar-coated asparagus. Spinach drops. Candy that is good for you. Children will clamor for it. Parents will be happy. Weight watchers will have a sweet that is good for them. Everyone will come here because *no one else is doing it.*"

Madeline thought about it for a minute. "You know,"

she finally said, "I can't believe I'm saying this, but it might just work."

"Girls, we need help," said Mildred. "There's a ton to be done. The charity fete is very soon."

Madeline and Katherine rolled up their sleeves. They were back in business!

Mrs. Bunny hopped up and down Main Street lazily, peering closely in shoppe windows she'd only glanced at before. She knew she should check on Mr. Bunny and the girls, but truthfully it was the first time she'd been alone in days and she was savoring it.

Bellyflop didn't have many shoppes, but their windows were all enticingly different. When Mrs. Bunny got to the bookstore she stopped. What she saw made her heart go pitter-patter. "Oh my goodness! Oh my goodness!" she muttered, panting, and sprint-hopped all the way back to the castle to tell Mr. Bunny.

# MR. BUNNY MAKES
## SOME FRIENDS

When Mrs. Bunny got to the castle she was still sprint-hopping as fast as she could. She couldn't *wait* to tell Mr. Bunny. But when she got to the bedroom where she should have found him napping, she instead found his note.

"Oh no, oh no," she said. Mr. Bunny had run off to go on the stage. And he *would* go at just such a time, when she had such exciting news. Still, she knew better than to try to find Mr. Bunny. When he had taken a theatrical turn it was best to leave him alone until it passed.

Instead she hopped back to the sweet shoppe. There she found the girls sweating profusely among the boiling sugar and vegetables.

"Girls, girls, guess what!" she said.

"What is it, Mrs. Bunny?" asked Madeline.

"What in heavens are you making here?" asked Mrs. Bunny, stopping to sniff the air. She was sure she caught a whiff of carrots.

"Vegetable candy. It's Flo's idea to make the shoppe pay. We're going to introduce it at the charity fete. We're going to invite everyone to the grand opening of Vegetable Candies. *The candy for the world citizen.*"

"What does that mean, the world citizen?" asked Mrs. Bunny.

"Flo doesn't know. It came to him in a dream," said Madeline.

"Hmmm, the confluence of vitamins and sugary comestibles?" asked Mrs. Bunny.

"Exactly," said Katherine.

"When is the charity fete?"

"Friday," said Katherine.

"Good," said Mrs. Bunny. "I could not help you on Saturday because I have a *BOOK SIGNING!*"

"Oh, Mrs. Bunny, how wonderful. Is there a bunny bookstore about?" asked Madeline, because she knew that human bookstores never seemed to ask Mrs. Bunny to sign books.

"No, it's the Bellyflop Book Shoppe that is having the signing. There's a poster saying the author of *Mr. and Mrs. Bunny—Detectives Extraordinaire!* and also the author of the latest ten-pound fantasy book, Oldwhatshername, would both be signing books on Saturday. I do pity Oldwhatshername. They shouldn't have two authors signing at the same time. It will be so embarrassing for her when everyone is lined up at my table and she has no one at hers."

Madeline looked worried. "But, Mrs. Bunny, why have the bookstore owners not informed *you* about the signing?"

"I suppose," said Mrs. Bunny, contemplating, "that they were shy. They put up the poster knowing I was in town. No doubt rumors have been rampant. This is what celebrity is, girls. And they hoped that if I saw the sign I would show up."

"It seems a lot to plan on the basis of hope," said Madeline doubtfully.

"Oh, Madeline, dear, you must always have hope," said Mrs. Bunny, clasping her paws rhapsodically in front of her heart. Her adrenaline was still pumping and it drove her to large gestures. She caught a glimpse of her reflection in the shoppe window. It was quite a fetching pose. Perhaps she would use it for her next author picture. "Someday I will write a book with such a winning theme. Such books seem to do well. Well, anyhow, I had better go through my suitcase and pick out a nice dress and shoes. Oh my, should I go right now to the bookstore and introduce myself or just show up the day of the book signing? Yes, I think that would be more dramatic."

"Hmmm," said Madeline. "What did Mr. Bunny think about all this?"

"He doesn't know. I'm afraid he has decided to go on the stage. It reminds me of the time he decided to join the circus. It was the tumbling that was his downfall."

"He couldn't tumble?"

"Well, he *could* tumble, it turned out. But it was never on purpose."

Then Mrs. Bunny rolled up her sleeves and put on an apron. It was all hands on deck.

Flo passed a tray of candy to Madeline, whose hands were already full, so Mrs. Bunny grabbed it. When Flo saw who he'd given the tray to, he gasped. But when he looked up Mildred was staring at him squint-eyed, so he said, "I don't see a rabbit. Nope. None. None at all."

"That's right," said Mildred. "We none of us do."

"I can work with rabbits without *believing* in them," said Flo uncertainly.

"That's right," said Mildred. "We all can."

And they did, for the rest of the afternoon and into the evening.

When Mrs. Bunny didn't return to the castle for dinner, Mrs. Treaclebunny hopped over to the sweet shoppe to find out what was keeping everyone. After they told her, she put on an apron to pitch in. Not because she wanted to be helpful, but to point out everything they were doing wrong.

"I don't see *two* rabbits now," said Flo.

"No," said Mildred. "You don't."

While the rest of his compadres were busy making chocolate beetroot and the like, Mr. Bunny had finally arrived at Stratford. The Royal Bunny Theatre was just letting out.

"Ah, the roar of the greasepaint," said Mr. Bunny contentedly, heading for the stage door. He was sure the actors would not mind him entering this way once they discovered he was one of them.

He hopped down a long corridor. A security bunny stopped him but Mr. Bunny waved him away with one of his recently acquired "Not now, my good mans." When done with the proper flick of the fingers, it was quite effective. Mr. Bunny finally found the dressing rooms. He knocked politely and then hopped in, saying, "It is I! The next Gielgud bunny."

He found the manly bunnies taking off their makeup with tissues and cold cream.

"Never did like Gielgud," said one.

"Gielbad is more like it," said another.

And then, to Mr. Bunny's consternation, they giggled.

Ah, said Mr. Bunny to himself, perhaps I was too quick to censor my own giggles. It seems to be a manly attribute, after all.

"Want to join the stage, do you?" asked one of the actors, swiveling his chair around. "Don't half get a dozen of you in here a week. American?"

"Canadian," said Mr. Bunny. When *would* people learn to tell the difference?

"Right. You'll have to give your life to it, then. Rehearsals all day and into the night. Then when we open, matinees and evening shows seven days a week. You'll have no time for family. One poor bloke tried to marry. That lasted two weeks. It's like becoming a monk, taking vows, giving up your worldly life. It's a devoted commitment, it is. Still sound good?"

"Yes, a devoted thespian bunny, I!" said Mr. Bunny, hoping they noticed the nobility of the pose he had struck.

"Right, then," said one of them. But Mr. Bunny heard him whisper to the actor next to him, "I give him ten days tops."

"Actually, I was only planning on it for a week. More or

less. Got to, uh"—Mr. Bunny cleared his throat and blushed—"get back to the wife. But I will be one hundred percent devoted while here, or, as I always say to Mrs. Bunny, 'I'll always be there—or thereabouts.'"

"Oh, well then!" said one of the actors. "I guess we're all in luck. One of our fellows has taken ill and can't come in the rest of the week. Course, it's rather a big part for a beginner. Guy has a bunch of troublesome daughters."

"King Lear?" asked Mr. Bunny, thinking, Be still, my beating heart. "My favorite Shakespeare play!"

"Righty-o. Come to the pub. We'll have a nice chitchat about it."

"Yes, it's beer and burp for all! I'm buying," said Mr. Bunny. Then he hoped they knew he only meant the first round.

He was very disappointed to find, when it came time to swagger up to the bar, that most of the actors were ordering crème de menthes and other little liqueurs. They drank them with their pinkies extended. It must be the theatrical way, he decided, and did the same. He did not really like the crème de menthe. It tasted like cough medicine but it was better than beer. He choked it down. After all, the next night he would be on the stage! A real Shakespearean actor, at last. And in the company of some spitting, brawling men for a change. Mrs. Bunny would be so proud of him. And then he got sad thinking of Mrs. Bunny. When he was away from her for more than ten minutes he missed her desperately. He wondered if she was sitting in the reclining chair watching *Say No to Those Pooey Wedding Dresses.* He had planned to show her those chairs. He wasn't sure she would find them on her own—wait a second—was that tall actor carrying a *purse?* No, it must be a manly sort of carryall. A special actory manly carryall for theatrical accessories. Very practical. He tried burping to fit in with his man friends, but crème de menthe tended to settle rather than excite the stomach. Oh well, thought Mr. Bunny, perhaps they'd all have a spitting contest soon. He sat patiently and waited.

The day of the school charity fete dawned bright and cheery. Mrs. Bunny was very excited as they set up their vegetable-candy booth. All across the school playing field were booths manned by various shoppes. There were balloons and jugglers and clowns and cotton candy, which here in England they seemed to call candy floss. They had the strangest names for things, thought Mrs. Bunny. Cotton candy looked nothing like dental floss. You certainly couldn't knit underwear out of it. But never mind; thanks to England, they would soon rake in the money and Madeline could go to college. It would all work out.

It was just too bad Mr. Bunny wasn't here to enjoy the success. No success ever had meaning to her without Mr. Bunny there to share it. Perhaps she should reconsider the cell phone. She would like to know that Mr. Bunny was okay. He had been gone three days. His theatrical turns usually only lasted a week. Then he got tired of staying up late at night. But this was no guarantee that he would be back in another four days. It might be longer this time! Mrs. Bunny might end up missing him so much she would lose her appetite. She would waste away to nothing. He would find her a pile of fur and bones. Hmmm, if that happened, she might fit into that slinky purple designer gown at Bunnydale's. But no, a cell phone was not worth it. It was a slippery slope. Before you knew it, you'd have bells and whistles going off in your pocket every second. "Mrs. Bunny must be *FREE*!" she said dramatically, and struck a pose. She was hoping some paparazzi would be around to capture it. She could just see the headlines—"Mrs. Bunny Strikes a Pose for Freedom." It would be good publicity for the book signing. Where were the paparazzi when you needed them?

Flo and Mildred stayed at the store stocking the shelves with cucumber clusters and eggplant fondant. They were expecting a huge wave of new customers as soon as people had sampled the vegetable candy at the charity fete. Katherine,

Madeline and Mrs. Bunny were left to man the booth. Mrs. Treaclebunny, who had originally planned to help out too, got sidelined by the duchess's invitation to join her in the day's hunt.

"They are planning a really *huge* hunt this week," Mrs. Treaclebunny had said excitedly that morning to Mrs. Bunny as they put on their fur gloss together.

Mrs. Bunny did not wear fur gloss every day, but she felt she must look her best for the charity fete even though she would not be seen underneath the booth. It was her job to hand Katherine the boxes and bows to pack the vegetable candy as the orders came in. They hoped they could manage with only one bunny's help. Mrs. Bunny worried about what would happen when word of the candy's vegetable goodness spread and people started pushing and shoving to get at it.

"A huge hunt?" Mrs. Bunny replied to Mrs. Treaclebunny. "That should be exciting, if damp. All those wet hedges. I would like to join you, but I am sure we will be so busy at the store they will not be able to spare me."

"It doesn't matter. You couldn't come anyway," said Mrs. Treaclebunny heartlessly. "Your title hasn't arrived yet. You can't do hunty-type things without a title. Mr. Bunny's has come in. He is to be Admiral Bunny as soon as he signs on the dotted line. And look, it comes with a hat."

Mrs. Bunny grabbed the white hat and Mrs. Treaclebunny looked at her suspiciously.

"I don't recall having seen admiral on the list of available titles," Mrs. Treaclebunny said.

"Well, I didn't see it either. But I wrote it down just in case. I said it was my first choice but if it wasn't available then I picked pharaoh."

"Well, they have written back to say that as a matter of fact, admiral is available but at highly inflated prices. In fact, twice the price. Oh, that's probably why your title hasn't arrived, Mrs. Bunny. It is probably because your check only covered admiral. You shall have to send another check, and you shall have to send it soon if you wish to work your way up to queen before we sail home."

"Yes, yes," said Mrs. Bunny. "I will hop to it and write another check immediately. *ADMIRAL.* How well that sounds. And it comes with accessories! Oh, Mr. Bunny *would* be gone to join the stage just when his admiral hat comes in! I am sure once he tries it on, he will want the full uniform!"

Mrs. Bunny told the girls this story as they all waited for their first customer. Families were now walking from booth to booth to buy things. All the booths were decorated with streamers, their paper fronts covered in pictures the schoolchildren had drawn. Now and then a balloon floated up to the summer sky. A dog ran by. There were strollers and women in hats and toddlers in face paint. For a second Madeline wished she and Katherine could join in the fun.

"What is happening?" asked Mrs. Bunny over and over. "It's very sweaty down here and I can't see anything except feet going by occasionally. Why is no one stopping at our booth?"

"I don't know . . . ," Madeline began when Mrs. Bunny heard Starlight Heavens's twangy Midwest tones.

"Vegetable candy? Sold any?"

"No," said Madeline and Katherine flatly.

"Whose idea was this? Mildred's, I suppose. Oh, darlings! There you are. Come meet some children of old friends. Ermintrude and Alfred, this is Madeline and Katherine."

There was a great deal of uncomfortable shifting of feet and Mrs. Bunny almost found herself stepped on.

"Ermintrude and Alfred can come up with arcane facts at the drop of a hat," Starlight Heavens said, breaking the awkward silence. "Give me a fact, Ermintrude."

"The nine-banded armadillo is a known carrier of leprosy," said Ermintrude.

"And Alfred?" prompted Starlight Heavens.

"Here is a Canadian fact for you. Perhaps you would care to proffer a guess as to the answer," said Alfred, who spoke through his nose and looked down it. "What is the highest mountain in Canada?"

"I don't know," said Madeline.

"I don't care," said Katherine.

"You poor children," said Starlight Heavens. "Because of your inferior schools, you aren't even taught your own history."

"That was geography, Mother," said Alfred.

"So it was. Bonus points to you!" said Starlight Heavens.

"The answer is Mount Logan," said Alfred. "It would be as well to know that, as perhaps you will hike there someday."

"Oh, Flo and Mildred don't hike," laughed Starlight Heavens.

"Yes, they do!" said Madeline. "They've taken me hiking a number of times."

"I don't think so," said Starlight pityingly.

"Mother, maybe what *they* call a hike is what *we* would call a long walk," said Alfred.

"Perhaps your parents are afraid of wild animals," said Ermintrude.

"My parents aren't afraid of anything," said Madeline.

"Your mother was terribly afraid to give birth to *you*," said Starlight Heavens. "She talked on and on about how frightened she was to go into labor. Poor woman. It's just another one of her neuroses."

"Now, Mother, many uneducated women are afraid of childbirth," said Ermintrude.

"That's true. We mustn't blame them. It's too bad that Denise couldn't be here today. We just got advance notice that if things continue as they do for little Ermintrude and Alfred, they will both be accepted to Oxford. Early. Before they are twelve!"

"Now, Mother," said Ermintrude. "You know we have to be at least fifteen."

"That's how old you have to be normally. But you are not normal."

"I'll say," whispered Katherine.

"Well, girls, at least there is no competition to get into Canadian schools. Aren't you lucky!" said Starlight Heavens. "Come, children, let's buy some chocolate-covered carrots to help these poor people so that someday, perhaps, little Madeline will be able to go to a provincial university."

"Oh, Mother, *nobody* could possibly want to go to one of those," said Ermintrude.

"Hush, dear," said Starlight Heavens, then whispered just loudly enough so that the girls could hear her, "They have no *choice.*"

Starlight Heavens bought three chocolate-covered carrots and gave one each to Ermintrude and Alfred. From under the booth, Mrs. Bunny saw the carrots drop at their feet as they walked off.

"OH!" she cried. "They threw them away. How dare they! What wretched people."

Madeline was so angry she could think of nothing at all to say. Instead she picked up a carrot herself and bit into it with sharp, angry bites. A second later she was spitting it out all over the field. "Oh my goodness," she said. "That's terrible. That's the worst thing I've ever eaten. Is all the vegetable candy this bad?"

"Shhh," said Katherine. "I think there's a customer coming."

After that, there was a steady trickle of customers and an even steadier sound of people spitting out chocolate-covered vegetables. By the end of the day the field was so covered with people's vegetable candy reactions that the grass itself looked chocolate-coated.

Flo and Mildred found themselves slipping and sliding on the debris as they arrived to help pack up.

"It's the darndest thing," said Flo. "Nobody came to the store at all. Nobody."

"But we used the time to make a lot more stock," said Mildred. "It's in the freezer."

"Throw it out," said Madeline. "And take down the sign. It's over. The store will fail."

"NO!" shouted Katherine, whose mother's cheerleading blood ran through her veins. "We must *FIGHT*. We must find *SOME* kind of candy people will buy. It's not over till it's over. It's always darkest before the dawn. You can't keep a good man down! Rah! Rah!"

She entertained them with a barrage of clichés all the way home. It didn't make Madeline feel any better, but it didn't make her feel any worse.

# MRS. BUNNY'S BIG DAY

Mrs. Bunny was perturbed. The vegetable-candy idea should have worked. Mr. Bunny had not returned from his stint on the stage, and Mrs. Treaclebunny was still out with the huge hedge hunt and was camping in a field overnight. The servants had all gone with the hunters to care for them. So Mrs. Bunny slept alone in the castle. I am not afraid of ghosts, she kept telling herself. I am *NOT* afraid of ghosts.

Flo was perturbed. Synchronicity seemed to be stalled. Go with the flow, he said to himself all night in his sleep. Go with the flow. In the morning he woke up quite refreshed.

Mildred was perturbed. This whole venture was turning into just another one of Flo's crackpot ideas. We should have just paved Canada in bottle caps, she thought petulantly. At least we wouldn't have Starlight Heavens crowing over our failures.

Katherine was perturbed. She found herself in this time of desperation becoming her mother. First it had been the rampant cheerleading. Now she was plagued by the irrepressible need to make a list. The problem was she didn't know what to put on it. She fell asleep with the pencil in her hand.

Madeline was perturbed too. Katherine was going to help Mildred and Flo in the shoppe while Madeline went to Mrs. Bunny's book signing with her. She still thought it strange that a store should be having a book signing without telling the author. It didn't seem right to her. She tossed and turned all night thinking about it.

But despite everyone's perturbation, the Saturday of the book signing dawned bright and fair. Mrs. Bunny was attired in her best black dress with the lace collar, her string of almost-real pearls and her black peep-toe pumps. She had a purple almost-alligator pocketbook over her forearm, and she had even put on a little fur gloss and taken out her quills for the day.

She met Madeline outside the bookstore.

"Look," she said proudly. "There's already a long line of people waiting for me. They snake right around the block. That should make the bookstore owners happy. Poor Oldwhatshername. I hope a few people buy her book just so she won't feel left out."

"Ye-e-es . . . ," drawled Madeline uncertainly. *She* had heard of Oldwhatshername. In fact, she was pretty sure everyone in the world had. Oldwhatshername obviously hadn't tapped into the bunny market yet, but it was only a matter of time. Oh dear, thought Madeline. Oh dear. She didn't know what might happen today, but she had a feeling it was not going to be good.

"Well, shall we?" asked Mrs. Bunny, going inside and marching up to the card table that was set up for her signing. But there a surprise met her. There was a woman already sitting there. Why, it was the translator of Mrs. Bunny's book!

"What are *you* doing here?" Mrs. Bunny asked her. "I suppose you have come to support me. How *kind,* how very *kind* of you!"

"Well, uh, yes," said the translator, looking uncomfortable. But then she always looked a little uncomfortable. "That and, uh, signing a few books."

"What books would those be?" asked Mrs. Bunny with perfunctory interest. She was getting very excited about her own signing. Her ears were twitching.

"Uh, you know, uh, your books."

*"Mr. and Mrs. Bunny—Detectives Extraordinaire!?"* asked

Mrs. Bunny in surprise, suddenly noticing the three huge stacks of her book in front of the translator. "How odd. But *you* didn't write it."

"I know, I know," said the translator hastily, picking lint off her clothes and those of anyone who came within reach. "I keep telling everyone that. But the thing of it is, Mrs. Bunny, they never seem to believe me. They think I'm joking. They ask me to sign anyway. They interview me anyway. It's as if . . . uh"—she paused, debating whether to tell Mrs. Bunny this—"they don't believe you exist!"

For a second Mrs. Bunny's ears shot up and made exclamation points on top of her head. *"DON'T EXIST?"* she squawked.

"Yes, I try to disabuse them but they think I'm . . ." And here the translator paused again. She did not like being the bearer of bad news. She was almost saintlike on her better days. "Lying. Or being, you know, overly cute. Humans, huh? That's why I live on an island. I figure it keeps most of them away. Unless they're, you know, very swimmy sorts."

"Oh well, I suppose it's not your fault," said Mrs. Bunny. "I'm here now, so you can just go home. Shoo. Shoo."

"Mrs. Bunny," whispered Madeline, "don't tell her to shoo." She turned to the translator, who was standing up and collecting her things. "She's just nervous, you know. She gets this way when she's nervous."

"Oh, that's quite all right, Madeline," said the translator. "I didn't want to be here anyway. I'd much rather be out shopping. I've been invited to the queen's annual tea party at Buckingham Palace, and as usual, I haven't a thing to wear."

"*You* were invited to have tea with the queen?" squealed Mrs. Bunny.

"Yes. You know, because of that bit in *Mr. and Mrs. Bunny—Detectives Extraordinaire!* about Prince Charles. I guess they found it flattering."

"But that's so unfair," said Mrs. Bunny. "I was the one who wrote that. And in the book it is I who says flattering things about Prince Charles, not you. What kind of dolt would attribute it to the translator?"

"Well, I think we've covered that subject . . . ," said the translator, looking more and more uncomfortable. She kept adjusting the straps of various undergarments and brushing randomly at her hair. "Anyhow, see your bunny publisher about it. Maybe they can snag you an invitation. The tea isn't for a few more days." Just then there was a great excitement outside and people standing in line began applauding.

"Oh, look," said Mrs. Bunny. "Here comes Oldwhatshername. No doubt they are applauding because she finally got here and now they can come in and get their bunny books signed."

There was a great fuss as the store owner led Oldwhatshername to her table. It was then that Mrs. Bunny noticed that Oldwhatshername's signing table was a priceless antique, not just some card table such as the one the owner had set up for the translator.

Never mind, said Mrs. Bunny to herself, do not be a diva bunny. Probably just trying to buoy Oldwhatshername's spirits as she sits quietly alone with no books to sign.

She tried smiling encouragingly at Oldwhatshername, who didn't seem to notice her. She had a sea of people swarming around her.

"Her entourage," said the translator bitterly.

"Well, someone from the shoppe should be paying attention. All the customers are getting in the wrong line," said Mrs. Bunny.

The people who had been outdoors were now rushing forward to be first at Oldwhatshername's table.

"Uh, apparently not," said the translator, and pointed. All the people had Oldwhatshername's latest fantasy novel in hand.

"WHAT?" said Mrs. Bunny. "Mrs. Bunny may faint. Have you any smelling salts? I cannot process such a bizarre turn of events. Has the world been turned upside down and set upon its long and fuzzy ear?"

"Well . . . ," said the translator, chewing on a cuticle and wishing she still smoked.

The bookstore owner, having Oldwhatshername comfortably settled, came over to Mrs. Bunny's table. "Oh my, *such* an exciting event has never before taken place in my shoppe," she said, looking (and smelling), thought Mrs. Bunny, extremely sweaty.

"Thank you," said Mrs. Bunny quietly.

Although the owner wasn't paying enough attention to hear Mrs. Bunny, she suddenly spied her on the chair next to the translator and broke into laughter.

"You brought a rabbit in costume!" she said between guffaws. "That's just hysterical! Now listen, dear, you're very lucky, being booked the same day that Oldwhatshername just happened to have an opening. She wasn't originally booked for this day, but when I found out she was willing to come, I said to her, come any day, come anytime at all. It is up to *us* to accommodate *you*. And I knew *you* wouldn't mind. However would you have seen so many faces here otherwise? Look at all the business she brought you! And you can bask in her reflected glory."

"Bask, bask," said the translator, scratching an arm and wondering if she had Lyme disease.

"Of course, at first they will all want to make sure they get Oldwhatshername's very, very special book signed, but afterward some will trickle over to see what your book is about."

The translator gave a sickly smile. She was doing her best to be polite and hoping very much she would not vomit on anyone's shoes.

Madeline squirmed uncomfortably. The owner suddenly noticed her.

"And I see you brought a young friend!" she said, and then turned to Madeline. "I bet you came hoping to meet Old-whatshername. But she's a very busy woman. Oh yes, a very busy woman."

"I'm here really for the bunny book," said Madeline. "*That's* the book I'm a fan of. And this is Mrs. Bunny, not just some stuffed—"

"Of course, of course," said the owner, winking at Madeline, and wandered away looking distracted and talking to her assistant. "Perhaps you should get Oldwhatshername some cookies? Does she eat cookies? She looks so very elegant and svelte. Most writers look like they spend their days eating potato chips and sticking their fingers in light sockets. My dear, when you've been in the business as long as I, the hairdos you'll see on some of them! Well, like that one." She pointed behind her hand at the translator, who was pretending not to hear and thinking she should never attend these things without a cyanide pill.

"Imagine being as beautiful as Oldwhatshername *and* so very successful. What a charmed life Oldwhatshername leads! But deserving, very deserving," said the owner, and wandered away to find something to tempt slim Oldwhatshername's capricious appetite.

"Charmed . . . ," echoed the translator, sighing and opening her purse, digging around until she found a half-gnawed chocolate bar and then shoving it unceremoniously into her mouth. Then she remembered Mrs. Bunny, who had also heard every word, and dug around some more. "Do you want something? I think I've got a practically whole caramel here somewhere."

"I don't understand any of this," said Mrs. Bunny. "Perhaps this is why I never seem to get any royalty checks from the human publisher. Even though I had been told my bunny book was selling like hotcakes in the human market."

"It's selling," said the translator glumly. "Not like hotcakes, maybe. Oh dear. I was going to tell you this, I just hadn't gotten around to it." She dropped her head on the table. "The publisher has been sending *me* the royalties. They think I wrote it, you know. They think you're . . . made up."

Mrs. Bunny just stared blankly.

"I haven't been *spending* them," explained the translator desperately. "I tried to have them converted to rabbit money immediately, but of course . . ."

"I know, I know. The carrot standard and the gold standard are not compatible," said Mrs. Bunny. She patted the translator's hand absently. This was a blow.

"Yes, but I opened a special bank account and I have put all your money there. I'm sure we'll find a solution eventually," said the translator.

"Not that it's ever the money that's the major thing. The disappointment, the humiliation . . . Oh, never mind," said the translator, and ate the half-chewed caramel herself.

She looked at Mrs. Bunny and sighed. It was painful to see such a brilliant writer as Mrs. Bunny slighted. But what could she tell her? Life is cruel, carry chocolate bars—that was her motto. "Ahem. Perhaps we should organize in case there *is* a trickle. I'll tell you what, Mrs. Bunny, you sit next to me and Madeline can page for us. Madeline, that means you open the book to the page Mrs. Bunny wants to sign. I'll sign it too, under the part that says *translated by.*"

"Yes, you must by all means sign too," said Mrs. Bunny kindly if patronizingly. "Since you *are* here and all. And it is such a *good* translation."

"I'm glad you think so," said the translator. "At least we can be each other's fans since we seem to have no others here."

They sat and twiddled their thumbs. They talked quietly among themselves. Mrs. Bunny and the translator exchanged recipes. Mrs. Bunny knew a very good recipe for carrot soup and the translator for an Asian salad that was to die for. Meanwhile, practically next to them, they heard people gushing and gushing to Oldwhatshername, who sounded graciously bored.

As the minutes dragged on and they had nothing to do, Mrs. Bunny said truculently to Madeline, "What makes her books so popular? That one has a very pooey cover."

"Oh, a bunch of wizards go to a British boarding school. There's magical happenings and stuff," said Madeline.

"Humph," said Mrs. Bunny. "*Anyone* can make up a good fantasy. Try writing a gripping realistic novel like *Mr. and Mrs. Bunny—Detectives Extraordinaire!* That's where the skill comes in!"

"What kind of magical happenings?" asked the translator, who hadn't read the books either.

"Oh, owls deliver letters."

"As if you could get an owl to deliver *anything,*" scoffed Mrs. Bunny.

"And the candy does magical stuff. Tricks."

"The candy does tricks? What kind of tricks?" asked Mrs.

Bunny, suddenly sitting up straight. Her ears formed two quivering question marks.

"Oh, there's candy that fills the room with bubbles and candy that makes you levitate. You know, that sort of thing."

"Hmmm," said Mrs. Bunny. "Madeline, grab one of those books and get in line!"

"WHAT?" said Madeline.

"Oh no, you haven't fallen under Oldwhatshername's spell too, Mrs. Bunny? Well, go ahead, the both of you. I'll just sit here by my lonesome and plan an early demise. Oh, I forget, that's no longer possible," said the translator gloomily, sinking lower and lower in her chair.

"I'm not interested in her *books*," said Mrs. Bunny. "I'm interested in her *candy*. Don't you see, Madeline? That's how we'll save the shoppe! What do people really want from a piece of candy? Not just its sugary goodness—they can get that from pie, for heaven's sakes, or a cookie. No, they want that something elusive. That hint of childhood wonders. They want MAGIC!"

She said this so loudly several of the people lined up in front of Oldwhatshername's table leaned over and said, "Shhhh!" They were trying to eavesdrop on what Oldwhatshername was saying to the patron in front of them.

"Oh, shhh yourself," said Mrs. Bunny. "Listen, Madeline.

Get in line and when it's your turn, ask Oldwhatshername how you get candy to do tricks, the way it does in her books. She must know. She wrote about it, after all. She must have done *some* research. And then tell her she got the owls all wrong. Wait a second, better hold off on that. Get the candy-training techniques first."

"Oh," said Madeline. "Do you think she'll tell me? Isn't that a trade secret or something?"

"Nonsense," said Mrs. Bunny. "If someone asked me for used-dental-floss knitting patterns, I'd be happy to oblige. Any decent rabbit would."

Madeline thought this might be where rabbits and humans differed, but she would give it the old college try. She would do anything for Mrs. Bunny. Even though, of course, Mrs. Bunny was doing this for her. She ran over to the table with the piles of books on it. She grabbed one and ran outside to take her place in line. But when Madeline was three people from the front, Oldwhatshername looked at her watch, turned to her personal assistant and whispered something.

The assistant stood up and said, "Ladies and gentlemen and children, I'm sorry to announce that Oldwhatshername must flee to her next event. She mustn't keep her fans waiting. Thank you all for coming!"

"NONONO!" cried Mrs. Bunny so despairingly that several people looked to see who had been stabbed.

"Don't worry," said the owner, who thought it was the translator who had screamed and came over to put a hand on her shoulder. "I put aside a signed copy for your little friend. A voice seemed to tell me she might not be quite so interested in your book as she pretended. Wasn't it nice of her to pretend so, though?"

"Oh, put a sock in it," said Mrs. Bunny, hopping out from under the table. She tried to snag one of Oldwhatshername's ankles as she walked by but was too late.

"*Do* something! Get up and trip her!" she said to the translator, who, having run out of chocolate, was experimentally nibbling on a little lint.

"Oh right, I've always kind of wanted to do that," said the translator, leaping forward but crashing to the floor because she was too late as well.

"Where's Madeline?" they asked each other, for they couldn't see her among the sudden melee of people trying to grab Oldwhatshername and detain her. Fortunately for Oldwhatshername, her personal assistant was a karate whiz and quite a few of the fans landed on the ground with dislocated bits and pieces.

Madeline, meantime, was in the back of Oldwhatshername's limo. The driver had gotten out to have a smoke and left the doors unlocked. When Oldwhatshername got in, Madeline said, "Hello. I just have one quick question."

"Better not let my personal assistant see you," said Oldwhatshername, who had just spied her assistant on the sidewalk heaving children over the car. "I keep telling her she has to stop throwing children." They looked out the window as people sailed across the car and into traffic. "What an arm, though. She ought to pitch cricket. All right. So you're one of those, are you?"

"One of whats?"

"Children who sneak into my limo while Sidney is having a smoke. It's not original, you know. I suppose you have something you want to ask me."

"Exactly," said Madeline.

"I'm not telling you how the series ends."

"I don't care. I've never read your books."

"Oh right," said Oldwhatshername, but looked as if she didn't believe her.

"I *haven't*. Really. But, of course, I know all about them. You can't escape that even if you want. And I just need to know about the magical candy. How do you get it to do those things? The tricks."

Oldwhatshername rolled her eyes. "And here I thought I'd been asked everything. Well, you must train it, of course. Consistent training is the answer. Just like with dogs."

"Thank you," said Madeline. She was preparing to alight from the limo when Mrs. Bunny, who was hopping madly outside searching for her, saw her opening the door and hopped over.

"I suppose you have a question too," said Oldwhatshername to Mrs. Bunny.

Mrs. Bunny's mouth opened. Was she *supposed* to have a question? What had Madeline been telling this woman? Was Madeline trying to delay Oldwhatshername with questions? She thought she'd better play along, so she asked Oldwhatshername the first question that came to mind. "Don't you really think the queen of England should be a rabbit?"

"Yes," said Oldwhatshername. "Now I really have to run." She tapped on the window at the driver. "Sidney, let's roll." Madeline barely had time to get out before the limo pulled away with a screech of tires. She fell into a man standing nearby who was scribbling in a notebook.

"Ah," said Mrs. Bunny to Madeline, pulling her off the man's foot. "Another writer. I must warn him, writer to writer." She looked up at the scribbling man and said, "A word of advice: don't do any book signings at *that* store. They don't know the difference between writers and translators. They don't even give you a *cookie*!"

But the man didn't seem to notice her, he just kept scribbling.

That night the headline in all the papers worldwide read, "Oldwhatshername Says She Thinks the Queen of England Should Really Be a Rabbit!"

Mrs. Bunny was soaking her tired-out-from-high-heeled feet and reading choice bits of the paper when she stumbled on this.

"Well," she said to herself. "Isn't that nice?"

Meanwhile, it was the second night *King Lear* was playing on the stage at Stratford. Mr. Bunny stood in the wings and peeked out at the audience. He had said many times that Mrs. Bunny had eyes that were always counting the house. If she had been here that was exactly what she would have been doing. But she wouldn't need to tonight. One look would tell her every seat was filled. And *he* was largely responsible. He had clipped the reviews from opening night and pocketed them to show Mrs. Bunny when he got home. "The most powerful Lear this company has seen yet!" read one. "This is a rabbit born to play Lear," read another. Yes. Wasn't that what he had always told Mrs. Bunny? Perhaps he would stay on to play the West End of London. Maybe he would take it on the road. A touring thespian bunny, he!

The play began. The other actors were swell players and terrific guys. They helped Mr. Bunny find his way onstage and off, pushing him hither and yon to hit his marks. They always insisted he come on last for the curtain call, and every man of them stepped back a bit so that he would be in the forefront for the bows. They had helped him learn his lines and practice them. They couldn't have been kinder. But nevertheless, as he stood onstage awaiting his next speech, his mind wandered back to Mrs. Bunny. He remembered the look on her face, her ears in a twist, as they waltzed shipboard. But what of his rising star? The romance of greasepaint and the open road? As he asked himself these questions, his happy dreams took an unexpected turn. Instead of the great adventure of the vagabond dramaturgic life, he saw himself returning each night to a lonely hotel room, eating store-bought carrot cake, darning his own socks, reading articles from *The Scientific Bunny* to no one, with no cheerful inane comments from Mrs. Bunny. He began to droop when suddenly he was awoken by a savage pinch.

"It's YOUR line," someone hissed at him.

"AND YET I HAVE A WIFE!" he thundered.

He did this so well that there was a sudden smattering of spontaneous applause.

"Daughter," hissed his fellow actor, "the line is 'And yet I have a *daughter*!'"

"That may be Lear's line but it is not mine," he whispered back. Then he bowed to the many whose clapping had become furious. Bunny clapping is not very loud. The fur muffles it. To compensate, it often goes on for quite a while. Mr. Bunny bowed again.

Then he hopped right off the stage.

# ▸TRAINING THE CANDY◂

The next day was to be a busy one. There was candy to train! Mrs. Bunny arose early and made her rabbity toilet before heading down the lonely echoey front stairs to have her coffee and toast. She almost shrieked her little bunny head off when she arrived in the kitchen and there sat a figure, his feet up on the table, reading the paper and crunching on some toast with carrot jam.

"I see there is talk about the queen of England being a rabbit. Did you have anything to do with this?" asked a certain lagomorphic pal.

"Mr. Bunny!" shrieked Mrs. Bunny, falling upon him with many furry hugs.

"Yes?" replied Mr. Bunny. "For so I am called."

"You have returned. How was life on the stage?"

"Oh, it had its moments, it had its moments," said Mr. Bunny, calmly crunching toast. "And look, the guys gave me this swell souvenir."

Mr. Bunny held out his brand-new manly carryall.

"They handed it to me as I hopped offstage midspeech."

"Midspeech? Weren't they angry to have you quit right in the middle of the play?"

"Oh no. Well, half of them were. The half that had bet fivers that I would leave you for a life on the stage. The half that had bet I'd be gone before the week was out were pretty happy. There was a slight delay in the play while the fivers changed hands and the understudy was brought on. But it's all part of the artistic life, my dear, all part of the artistic life. Here, look at my reviews. They call me masculine and full of dash."

"Well, of course you're masculine. And full of something."

"Dash."

"Whatever."

"Anyhow, I did give that speech a stirring reading. 'AND YET I HAVE A DAUGHTER!'" thundered Mr. Bunny in his best stentorian voice, hopping up to stand on the chair for effect.

"Oh, Mr. Bunny," said Mrs. Bunny admiringly, but not really paying attention because she was busy exploring all the pockets of the manly carryall.

"Yes, I was quite the theatrical hit, Mrs. Bunny."

"You may as well give me the bag," said Mrs. Bunny thoughtfully. "I don't believe you look so dashing carrying a purse as you might think."

"It's not a purse," said Mr. Bunny.

"It is now," said Mrs. Bunny, transferring all the contents of her old purse into her new one. "It's enough for you that you had your turn on the stage. And I know you; you would soon tire of this thing and lose it. Now, I am going to have a quick breakfast, and then we must hop to the sweet shoppe. It is a good thing you returned when you did. We have much to do." And she filled him in on the new plan to teach candy to do magical things. "Training, consistent training. Just like with dogs."

The Bunnys hopped all the way into Bellyflop holding paws. They had missed each other something terrible.

At the sweet shoppe all was hustle and bustle. Madeline had told everyone about Mrs. Bunny's magical-candy idea. Of course, to Flo and Mildred she had claimed the idea as her own. They all thought it was brilliant, so Flo painted a new sign for the shoppe. It said:

MAGICAL CANDY

JUST LIKE IN OLDWHATSHERNAME'S BOOKS!

Katherine had made a list of all the tricks they could teach the candy. The bubble gum was to blow to the size of a hot-air balloon, and the blower would be able to hang from it by her teeth and float away. The string licorice was to grow to great lengths, to be tossed around tree branches so you could swing from them. The jawbreakers would turn you different colors as you sucked through the layers. First red, then blue, then yellow. Who *wouldn't* want to be an exciting shade of puce now and then?

There were two dozen types of candy set out on the shelves, all needing to be trained. It was quite exhausting. By the end of the day all they had achieved were bubble gum bubbles that blew up to the size of regular balloons. But Madeline said she wasn't sure anyone would call this magical. Also the bubbles refused to float up into space and it was quite a mess when they popped.

"Don't worry," said Mrs. Bunny. "When have you ever had a puppy you could train in a day? It takes time and patience."

"We may have patience but we don't have time," said Madeline. "We're already into August and we have made no money

at all. We have *lost* money. Flo says he has gotten a gig on a cruise ship leaving in ten days. We have *ten* days to make thirty thousand dollars, Mrs. Bunny. We must open the shoppe to-morrow and hope for the best."

Mr. Bunny was just about to say someone might have consulted him before starting such a ridiculous project, when Madeline added, "Oh, Mr. Bunny, you must put your big brain to work! It's our only chance!"

It melted his little bunny heart. "Yes, ahem, you can al-ways count on that," he replied. "Come, Mrs. Bunny. Let us hop-pace back and forth; you know how that always jogs my brain into action."

Mr. and Mrs. Bunny hopped back and forth in front of the store. Occasionally Mrs. Bunny, who wasn't blessed with Mr. Bunny's focus, broke into a cha-cha.

"Concentrate, Mrs. Bunny!" barked Mr. Bunny. "I am al-ways on the verge of a big idea when you distract me with your dancing fur."

But unfortunately, in the end Mr. Bunny's long hopping journey the night before had rendered him unfit for more than fifteen minutes of hop-pacing. His paw pads were bruised and weary.

"We must make our adieus," he said to Madeline and

Katherine. "But fear not, I will set my big bunny brains to boil and they will churn through the night with so many ideas that you will not be able to keep up."

And then he and Mrs. Bunny hopped back to the castle and bed. He was snoring before his head hit the pillow.

In the morning the Bunnys found Katherine and Madeline looking cross and tired. They had stayed up most of the night trying to train the candy.

"But we did it. Mostly," said Madeline, yawning. "Look."

She shook out a piece of licorice. It did look as if it might be a tiny bit bigger.

"Okay, it's not great, but it *is* magical," said Madeline, looking hopeful.

"It took all night just to get it to do that," said Katherine. "This is impossible. We'll never have it ready in time. People will call us charlatans. The shoppe will go bankrupt. Mildred will never have the money to buy the vegetable garden and Madeline will never have the money to go to college. She'll be living in a grass hut and making silver jewelry until the day she dies."

"Why a grass hut?" asked Mr. Bunny. Nothing got past his big bunny brain.

"Now listen," interrupted Mrs. Bunny. "You must never think that way. After all, everything has worked out so far. I think you've done a lovely training job and I'm sure you've planted the *idea* in the candy's head. It's just like training a puppy. You say, 'Sit, sit, sit, sit' until you're blue in the face and you think they will never understand and then one day they do it just like that and you realize it just needed time to sink in. I'm sure the candy will think about its trick on the way home in the brown bag, and once it reaches its destination it will all be clear in its head and it will snap to and start performing. After all, what else does it have to do with its time?"

"Mrs. Bunny, you're sounding daft," Mr. Bunny whispered in her ear.

"Hush!" Mrs. Bunny whispered back. "Look at Madeline's face. She must have hope." Then she turned back to the girls. "Just think, you saved the day even without Mr. Bunny's big brain. Good for you!"

While Mrs. Bunny continued to make her usual encouraging noises, Mr. Bunny quietly took one of each kind of candy behind the shoppe to see what the girls had achieved. It was frighteningly little. Mr. Bunny saw lawsuits and debt and ruin ahead. But never fear, he said to himself, now that his enormous bunny brain had had its full quota of refreshing sleep, it was grinding out ideas at its usual stunning rate. There were six or seven stacked up in the hopper already. He chose number four.

"Mrs. Bunny," he said, pulling her aside after he'd hopped back into the shoppe. "This whole venture is going to go bust without our help."

"I feared as much," whispered Mrs. Bunny. "Oh dear, oh dear, oh dear. What are we to do?" She said this while wringing her fur. When she discovered that this pinched, she grabbed hold of Mr. Bunny's and wrung his instead.

"Stop that!" he said, slapping her paw.

"Ow, stop that yourself!" she said, slapping him back.

"Get ahold of yourself. As usual, I have a plethora of ideas. I have selected idea number four to begin with. We are going to write out the training techniques for each kind of candy on a sticky label, and as the customers leave the shoppe, you and I will surreptitiously stick the labels on the bags. You know how no one ever notices us. We can pretend to be statues standing right inside the door. No one will suspect we are alive."

"Why would there be statues right inside the door?" asked Mrs. Bunny skeptically. "I see many flaws in this plan, Mr. Bunny."

"Shut up. There just would. We are no longer selling trained candy—we are selling people the fun of training their own! Of course, once people start crowding to get in the shoppe, we will have to be careful no one steps on us or mistakes us for earmuffs."

"Nobody could ever mistake you for an earmuff," said Mrs. Bunny placidly. "You are far too noisy and opinionated."

There was always a honeymoon period after the Bunnys had been separated but it never lasted long. Mr. Bunny could see this one was already over.

"Humph," he said, and they hopped back to the castle to use the duchess's computer and printer to make millions of sticky labels spelling out the training technique for each kind of candy.

It was a very busy week but quite an exciting one. A shoppe with magical candy. Who could resist? First the news of the magical-candy shoppe spread by word of mouth. Even parents who did not normally allow their children candy came to sneak a peek. And once inside, how could they resist buying?

"Look, Bertha," said a man with six drooling children in tow. "Jelly beans that turn into tropical fish when you drop them in the bath! Bubble gum that blows bubbles the size of hot-air balloons. We'll have one of each kind of candy you've got," he said to Mildred, who was busy serving six other people as well.

"But, Fred," said Bertha, "we never give the children candy. You say you can't afford the dental bills."

"Look, they've got dollies that turn into REAL dollies! For fifty pence each. That's very good value, Bertha. You can't buy the girls dollies for fifty pence. We could buy dozens and open a dolly shoppe. Give me all your dollies!" he barked at Mildred, who was looking exhausted and confused by the crowds waiting outside and shouting for others to hurry and finish their business so they could have a turn.

"Hey, that's not in the spirit of the shoppe," said an irate woman. "You can't take *all* the dollies!"

"Just watch me!" said Fred.

"Oh, let him," said the irate woman's husband. "I want all the jellies that become tropical fish. I'm going to start an aquarium."

"Don't worry, there's more in the back, always more in the back!" said Flo happily. He was astounded to find that one of his business ventures was finally successful. "And it's all thanks to Oldwhatshername!"

"How's that again?" asked a man who was a reporter for a local paper and happened to be in the shoppe buying some exploding gumdrops. He got out his notebook and pen and started scribbling.

Soon every newspaper in the country carried the story, which brought in yet more customers. And with them, more reporters.

Finally, a tabloid printed a story that Oldwhatshername had gotten word that her name was on a shoppe sign and was suing! Oldwhatshername had retired to her castle with eau de cologne on her forehead from the shock of being so used!

"'I Invented Magical Candy!' Says Oldwhatshername," read the headline. At first Flo and Mildred were concerned.

"We cannot afford to be sued," said Mildred.

But before Flo and Mildred had a chance to worry in earnest, it was revealed that the tabloid had made the story up. Oldwhatshername neither knew nor cared about the shoppe. When asked about it in an interview she said, "Sue? Nonsense, I wish them luck."

Whether for good or bad, the tabloid story brought in yet more people.

Mr. and Mrs. Bunny were kept very busy sticking on labels and trying not to be noticed. They had to quickly develop the technique of selecting the proper labels for each person's candy bag and hopping up and sticking them on as the customers left the shoppe. Although the candy wasn't magical, the labels themselves began to create new interest in the shoppe.

"There was nothing on the bag when they handed it to

me!" customers told their friends. "But when I got home, these training directions appeared. Like magic! I can't get the candy to do tricks, but the shoppe is magic, all right. How else could the labels with the magical directions suddenly appear?"

"It's not magic, it's a miracle!"

"It's not a miracle, it's magic."

The newspapers started up again. "Magical Happenings in Bellyflop." "The Mystical Appearance of Labels on Bags!" Flo was interviewed and mystified everyone by repeating over and over, "It's just like what happened with the Pop-Tarts. It's the mystical appearance of sugar in all our lives!"

"The things people will believe," said Mr. Bunny in disgust. "Magical mystical, indeed. A lot of hard work by bunnies is more like it."

"People need magic," said Mrs. Bunny. "They need to believe in such things."

"Pshaw!" said Mr. Bunny.

As yet more and more people came in and out of the shoppe, Mr. and Mrs. Bunny had a hard time keeping up with sticking the labels on the bags. Oftentimes they missed someone until the person had left, and had to hop down the street after him on their long and floppy tired shoppe feet.

So it was one day just as the shoppe was closing. The last two customers managed to slide out with unlabeled bags.

"I'm going to have a heart attack if this keeps up," said Mr. Bunny as he and Mrs. Bunny went hopping wildly after them. Unfortunately, the couple got on a motorbike and sped off. Mr. and Mrs. Bunny, without a thought, followed swiftly behind.

They could see the couple getting off their motorbike on a distant hill and strolling through the meadows. "Come on," said Mrs. Bunny wearily. "They're on foot again. We can catch up."

The Bunnys finally came upon the couple under a tree, their bag unattended, so it was the work of a moment to label it. They were trying to roll down the hill to give their paws a rest when Mrs. Bunny found herself suddenly next to a largish hole with a fox speeding toward it.

"Shoot it! Shoot it! Before it makes its way through its foxy tunnel!" cried a voice, and looking up, Mrs. Bunny saw a large band of hedgehogs on horseback racing toward her. The speaker threw a gun to Mrs. Bunny, who caught it deftly.

"Shoot the fox?" said Mrs. Bunny in confusion. "I thought you were on a hunt for hedges?"

"Don't be stupid," cried the Duchess of Bungleyhog. "Hurry. Shoot it before it gets away. Shoot it and we'll make you queen!"

Mrs. Bunny looked down the hole. The fox had caught his tail on a root. He peered up at her and the gun. His face turned pale as he saw his fate approaching.

"Hurry up! He'll get away. We've been hunting him for days. This is your chance. You'll be queen in a trice! You can skip all the social-climbing preliminaries. Now SHOOT!" yelled the duchess.

Mrs. Bunny leaned into the hole and took aim. She could be queen!

The fox was so frightened he turned his head and threw up all over his nice plaid pants.

"Oh dear," said Mrs. Bunny faintly. "That was messy."

She jumped down the hole and untangled his tail from where it had caught on the root. "Run!" she said quietly. "Run."

The fox took one short, scathing look at her and, with a "So long, sucker," dashed off down his tunnel.

Mrs. Bunny climbed out of the hole. She was sweaty and dirty and her fur was in disarray. The hedgehogs sat on horseback in a circle around the hole, glaring down at her. Mrs. Bunny was so fed up she had the strength of ten bunnies. She looked defiantly at all those high-up-on-the-social-ladder hedgehogs, broke the gun in half and shoved the pieces down the hole.

"I think you're all cracked," she said. "Come on, Mr. Bunny. Let us find a good B and B."

Later that evening at the British Bunny B and B, Mr. and Mrs. Bunny were soaking their feet in lavender water. Mr. Bunny did not like the scent but told Mrs. Bunny he was willing to put up with anything if she would just refrain from telling the story of the time she almost shot a fox. Six times was too many.

"Seven's a charm," said Mrs. Bunny, who became more saintly with each retelling. In the seventh she planned to put in a bit where bunnies, hearing her tale, erected shrines to her up and down the countryside, where they would leave carrots and other choice vegetation. She was particularly fond of this part and was enthusiastically relating it to Mr. Bunny when she was interrupted by Mrs. Treaclebunny, who had just arrived and was heard below having a loud argument with the landlady about the room rate.

"Drat that woman," said Mr. Bunny. "Can we never lose her even for one night?"

"I suppose," said Mrs. Bunny to Mrs. Treaclebunny as she popped her head into the Bunnys' room without knocking, "that you aren't too pleased with me right now."

"Aw, I was getting sick of wearing quills anyway," said Mrs.

Treaclebunny, who hopped in as Mrs. Bunny was adjusting the fire and took over her chair. "Not to mention the food on the hunt. Does nobody know the proper way to use a brazier? And sleeping in tents is not all it is cracked up to be."

"The duchess, then. She wasn't too pleased, I take it."

"All in a day's work for a duchess, that's her attitude. There was a certain amount of grumbling, of course, along the lines of what can you expect from Canadians. Horrible snobs, hedgehogs."

"Duh," said Mr. Bunny.

"Oh, and they did mention that now you'll never be queen. They'll be sure to see to that."

"I thought as much," said Mrs. Bunny, and a tear dripped down her cheek.

"Stuff and nonsense," said Mr. Bunny. "How do they figure it's all up to them?"

"That's on their family crest. Right beside *No Problems, No Dilemmas, Many Hedges. It's All Up to Us.* And, of course, they made me give back our titles. And they didn't even give us a refund."

"Oh no," said Mrs. Bunny. "And mine hadn't even arrived yet!" And then she remembered something else. "And I forgot to take Mr. Bunny's admiral hat with us!"

"All in all, the whole thing was a colossal waste of money,

just as I said from the start. It is just as well you didn't bring the hat, Mrs. Bunny," said Mr. Bunny. "I would never have worn it anyway."

"So you say," said Mrs. Bunny under her breath. She wondered if she could find him one in a shipboard gift store on the journey home.

"Anyhow, I was getting tired of the fox hunt. All that jumping things on horseback. It rattles your insides. Bad for the kidneys, that's what I say."

"And here I thought you were hunting hedges," said Mrs. Bunny.

"Hunting hedges? You don't hunt hedges. You *steal* hedges. Now, what are we doing after dinner? I've loads of energy still. We've done practically no sightseeing. And I've a list right here of enticing tourist traps. If we hurry we can knock off seven or eight by sundown."

For the first time in their acquaintance, Mr. Bunny silently led Mrs. Treaclebunny to the hall and shut the door behind her. Then he locked it. Then he went to bed. Mrs. Bunny followed shortly after.

It was very quiet in the room.

Mrs. Bunny was not sure what mood had befallen Mr. Bunny. Was he miffed at being left out of her tales of bunny sainthood? She supposed she could always put him in as a kind of Sancho Panza bunny figure. She had a feeling, though, he would not be satisfied to be cast as such. Should she ask him what ailed him? No. After many years of marriage she knew sometimes ignorance was bliss. "Would you like a chocolate biscuit?" she asked instead.

"No."

"They have some plain ones too in this tin by the bed."

"I would like some sleep."

"Well. It's been a long day. A long, still-not-a-queen day. Oh my," she sighed.

Mr. Bunny did not try to console her. His eyes were squeezed shut. Nope, no help for me there tonight, she thought.

"Well, anyhow, bunny pals forever?" she ventured.

Mr. Bunny put his paw in hers, and perhaps he was merely tired, for soon they were both in such deep slumber there was no room for dreams.

Mrs. Bunny woke up later in the night and ate three chocolate biscuits. She found sainthood gave her a tremendous appetite. And she approved of cookies by the bed. It was one thing the British got right. "We shall keep that in the repertoire," she said sleepily to herself, and in minutes was back asleep.

# ⇥TEA WITH . . . . . . . . . THE QUEEEEEEN!!!!!⇤

It was on day eight. At two o'clock exactly. The shoppe was packed as usual. Mr. and Mrs. Bunny were perspiring freely among the knees.

"What is the dewiness that is the opposite of failure?" asked Mr. Bunny.

"Mr. Bunny, you know how I feel about riddles," said Mrs. Bunny.

"I'll give you a clue. Not flop sweat but . . ."

"*HOP* sweat!" said Mrs. Bunny, demonstrating by hopping up to stick a label on another departing bag. "HAHA-HAHAHA!" She did not like to encourage Mr. Bunny in his riddledom, but even she recognized a good one when she heard it. Just as she was on her fifth ha, she heard the till slam closed and Flo shouted, "THAT'S IT! We did it! Converted from pounds, we've made thirty thousand dollars! And not a minute too soon. Our ship sails at the end of the week. Let's close the shoppe!"

"NO!" shouted all the unserved customers. "Not fair! Our turn!"

"Really, Flo," said Mildred. "It wouldn't hurt to have a little extra. . . ."

"Oh no," said Flo. "We're not going shipboard shopping. We're not doing *that* again."

"No, but certainly we need transport to the ship and from the ship to Hornby when we get back to Victoria," said Mildred.

"Oh. Right. But after we earn that, we are done. You know what that means, don't you?" asked Flo.

"College!" said Madeline.

"Veggies for the people!" said Mildred.

"No, man, I mean, for the cats! The *cats*!" said Flo.

So, though jubilant and exhausted, they kept the shoppe open for the rest of the day.

*   *   *

There was a party atmosphere for the last few hours in the shoppe. Somehow reporters had already found out about its closing. Headlines read, "Owner Says Now the Cats Have a Chance!"

At five o'clock, just as the Bunnys thought their paws were going to give out, the door tinkled one last time and in came Starlight Heavens, Alfred and Ermintrude.

"Hey, Starlight, candy on the house," said Flo. "We made our thirty thousand and we're splitting."

"I'm going to college!" said Madeline. She wasn't saying this to Starlight specifically. She'd been repeating it happily like a mantra all day in the shoppe. She couldn't seem to stop.

"Oh, this was to make you money for college, was it, dear? I must say I knew Canadian colleges were cheap. I didn't know they were *that* cheap. I suppose it reflects the *level* of education."

Mildred was busy closing up the shoppe, so she handed Madeline the mail to open. Madeline tried to ignore Ermintrude, who was explaining in detail what made Oxford superior to Harvard. After all, what did Madeline care? She would go *somewhere* to college now. That was all she wanted.

Madeline came to a thick cream envelope. "What's this?" she asked.

"If it's some lawyer telling us someone left us another business, forget it," said Flo. "I've been working steady the whole month of August. I need a year's break at least."

"It's not a letter from a lawyer. It's . . . it's from Queen Elizabeth!" said Madeline.

"Oh man, first Prince Charles comes to Comox, then the queen starts writing us. Why won't those people leave us alone?" said Flo.

"Why, we're invited to a tea party with her," said Madeline.

"Gack. That's why social excuses were invented," said Flo. "Tell her, like, we have a dentist appointment that day."

"*You're* invited to a tea party with the queen?" said Starlight, grabbing the invitation out of Madeline's hand and reading it herself. "*YOU?*"

"Why, yes," said Madeline. "She says here that our magical-candy making has uplifted the British people's spirits."

"Hey, it was just synchronicity and the universe, man," said Flo. "Like, we can't really take credit."

"Oh, yes we can," said Madeline and Katherine.

"Besides," said Katherine. "Prince Charles has already met Madeline. He gave her her awards when he came to our school's graduation ceremony. He talked to her more than anyone!"

"Oh really?" said Ermintrude nastily. "But I suppose you can't remember exactly what he said?"

"He admired my shoes," said Madeline.

"But, of course, you can't go," said Ermintrude, pretending to ooze sympathy. "Your parents are going to pretend to have a dentist appointment."

"Nonsense," said Madeline, looking Ermintrude in the eye. "We wouldn't miss this for anything in the world."

Then, catching sight of the Bunnys in the corner grinning, she smiled right back. But she wasn't the only one to see the grinning Bunnys this time.

"There's a couple of rabbits smiling over there!" said Ermintrude.

"No, there's not," said Starlight Heavens, and hustled her children out of the shoppe.

"But I saw them too!" said Alfred as they walked to their car.

"No, you didn't!" said Starlight Heavens. "Our sort doesn't see smiling rabbits. What has gotten into you? That's what you get from rubbing elbows with the riffraff."

"But they're having tea with the queen. Why don't we ever get to have tea with the queen?"

"Oh, put a sock in it," said Starlight.

And that was that.

The next day everyone went out and bought appropriate tea party clothes. At the suggestion of the dress shoppe owner, Mildred, Katherine and Madeline bought large gaudy hats as well. Fortunately, Mrs. Treaclebunny and Mrs. Bunny had packed hats.

"How I do wish Mr. Bunny could wear his admiral's hat," bemoaned Mrs. Bunny.

"Oh well, the men don't wear hats at these things," said Mrs. Treaclebunny. "It's mostly just the women."

"I'm sure the admirals wear hats," said Mrs. Bunny.

"Mr. Bunny is not an admiral," said Mrs. Treaclebunny. "We none of us have titles now, nor will we. Thanks to you know who."

This was really very cruel and Mrs. Bunny began to cry. Mr. Bunny, who was putting on his tuxedo and trying to stuff in the errant tufts of fur, came at a run.

"I'm very happy that Madeline is to go to college," said Mrs. Bunny, sniffling. "I am so happy about that that I feel very selfish, but I did so want to come home a . . . a . . . *queen.*"

"Well, well, you are *meeting* one," said Mr. Bunny, patting her on the back. "You will have to be content with that."

"It is not the same," sobbed Mrs. Bunny. "It is not the same at all."

"Mrs. Bunny, we have to go in ten minutes," said Mr. Bunny. "Please refrain from dripping on my cummerbund."

Mrs. Bunny recovered herself enough that when Madeline and Katherine came to collect them at the B and B, you could not tell that Mrs. Bunny had been crying. She had a damp patch or two of fur. That was all.

"Here, dears," said Mrs. Bunny. "I was going to give you these when the ship landed as end-of-summer presents but I thought you could use them today."

She gave each girl a shawl knitted from used dental floss.

"I knit them in the evenings."

"Oh, thank you," said Madeline. "What are these little orange things? Beadwork? Oh. Carrot bits."

Katherine said nothing but stared bug-eyed at her shawl.

She must be so grateful she is at a loss for words, thought Mrs. Bunny happily.

When they reached Buckingham Palace they were startled to find the grounds covered with people in tea party clothes.

"Well!" said Mrs. Bunny. "I rather thought we were having a private audience. But the queen seems to have invited a *great* many people to this little shindig of hers. Surely they haven't *all* contributed to Britain's high spirits. The British didn't look *that* ecstatic to me. We'll never meet the queen at this rate. Why, she could be anywhere in this crowd."

"That's why it pays to be knee-high," said Mrs. Treacle-bunny. "We'll cut through these nebbishy sorts in no time, case the joint, find the royal mucky-mucks and come back for *this* lot." She cocked her head at Mildred, Flo, Madeline and Katherine, who were looking around with stunned expressions. "No sense waiting for Queen Elizabeth to come to you—go to Queen Elizabeth, that's what I always say. Then have a few scones and chompies and head home. Come on. Hop to it, you two."

Mrs. Treaclebunny was right. Because they could hop about beneath and between the crowd, they quickly located the queen. She was standing with Prince Philip, Prince Charles and somebody whose job seemed to be to usher people in and out of her royal presence.

"That's the majordomo," said Mrs. Treaclebunny knowledgeably.

The bunnies raced back to get Madeline and Katherine, who had no trouble steering Flo and Mildred in the direction of the queen. But when they got there they found that the majordomo paid no attention to them at all. Even when Mr. Bunny bit him slightly on the ankle.

"Stop that," hissed Mrs. Bunny. "Do you want to get us thrown out?"

"I'm just trying to get his attention," said Mr. Bunny, biting the majordomo again. But he didn't even look down.

They all drifted around shyly for half an hour after that, always close to the royals and the majordomo, while other people were selected and brought over to the queen.

Then a little bell rang. It was time for everyone to make for the tents for refreshments. The majordomo began to steer the royals away.

"Well, that's that," said Madeline. But just as Prince Charles was moving off, he stopped. He turned and gave Madeline and Katherine a long and searching look.

Then he headed toward them.

"He remembers me!" whispered Madeline to Katherine.

"I say," said Prince Charles. "I was just admiring your shawls. You know, I saw a very similar pair of shoes once. Knitted by a rabbit out of used dental floss."

The majordomo followed Prince Charles. At this last remark he rolled his eyes. Could they never get the prince to keep his yap shut?

"Sir, perhaps you would like to move toward the tent," he said.

"Oh yes, do let me take you over to meet Their Majesties," said Prince Charles to the girls.

"And my mother and father," said Madeline, grabbing Flo and Mildred, who were drifting about overwhelmed by the crowd.

"And our rabbit friends," said Madeline, looking down. "I was the girl in the dental floss shoes. And Mrs. Bunny knit them. She's right here. And this is Mr. Bunny and Mrs. Treacle-bunny."

Prince Charles looked down. "How delightful! I've always been a big fan of your work," he said to Mrs. Bunny, reaching down to shake her paw.

Mrs. Bunny blushed and blushed and Mr. Bunny, for once, was at a loss for words. He was never surprised that he himself appreciated Mrs. Bunny, but he was quite astonished when anyone else did.

They moved as a group over to the queen, where the major-domo made the formal introduction.

"The royalty are seeing rabbits," whispered Flo to Mildred. "Is it okay to see rabbits when royalty sees them too?"

"No," hissed Mildred. "Don't you get it? *Us* seeing royalty seeing rabbits is part of *our* flashback."

"Heavy," said Flo.

When she got in front of the queen, Mildred forgot to curtsy but she did manage a stuttered, "Y-you're the *queen*!"

"So I've been told," said Queen Elizabeth.

Flo alone retained his savoir faire, stuck out his hand and said, "I once had a dog named Elizabeth!"

Madeline and Katherine were introduced next and they

both remembered to curtsy, although they could think of nothing to say. For years afterward Katherine would wake up in the middle of the night remembering that she once met the queen of England and all she could do was make gulping noises.

Mrs. Treaclebunny was completely agog when it came her turn. All her normal superiority had left her when faced with a real queen. "Oh, how I wish my poor nothing-left-but-the-desiccated-liver husband could be here for this!" she exclaimed.

Queen Elizabeth and Prince Philip stared at her blankly.

"I hate it when Charles invites these ventriloquist acts to these things," Prince Philip hissed to the queen. "The thing I can't figure out is which one of them is making it talk. Can't we have a rule about no more puppets?"

Mr. Bunny muscled up and said, "Charmed, charmed. Now if you could just point us in the direction of the tea cakes? I hear there are some very nice jammy ones. Quite a spread you put on here, quite a spread."

Mrs. Bunny watched all the others go before her. She did not know what she would do when she advanced in front of the queen, but she had certainly better think of something to redeem their party. What should she say? Something sophisticated. Something intelligent and arresting. Something to forever impress upon Her Majesty the suave wit of the rabbit. When it was her turn she hopped forward and did a little hop-curtsy. And then, before she was even aware of it, her mouth opened and what came out was "BUT *I* WANT TO BE QUEEN!"

The majordomo broke in at that moment and shuffled the queen and Prince Philip off while a team of security guards, all dressed in summer suits to blend in, took Mrs. Bunny away for questioning. What could Madeline, Katherine and Mr. Bunny do but hop after them? Mrs. Treaclebunny headed for the tea cakes. "After all, I tried to warn her," she told herself, even though she had not. "And those jam cakes look like they're going fast."

Mrs. Bunny found herself in a room in Buckingham Palace with a bunch of mean-looking burly men glaring at her.

"It must have a hidden microphone in it," said one of the security men.

"Maybe it's a bomb cleverly disguised as a talking rabbit," said another.

Oh dear, she thought. Does this presage dogs or the soup kettle? Or laboratory experiments? When mean humans got ahold of you it could come to any number of bad ends. But just as she was about to faint, the door opened and in came Prince Charles and Mr. Bunny.

"You can leave her to me," said Prince Charles. The security guys left immediately but they looked very disappointed.

"I am so sorry. What a frightful thing to have happen," said Prince Charles. "I've sent the girls off for their tea cakes. The jam ones tend to go fast. Now, what can I do to make up for this dreadful misunderstanding?"

"Make me queen?" asked Mrs. Bunny in a small voice.

Prince Charles thought for a second. "I can't do that, I'm afraid. There is one already, you see."

"Maybe there could be two?" asked Mrs. Bunny.

"Mrs. Bunny—" said Mr. Bunny in warning tones.

"No, no," said Prince Charles to Mr. Bunny. "She has a right to ask for splendid compensation. It must have been frightful to be dragged in here like that. Now there can't be two queens, kind of defeats the point of a monarchy and out of my jurisdiction completely, but I *could* knight you. Both of you. You could be Dame and Sir Bunny."

Mrs. Bunny thought for a second. "What about king?"

"For him?" asked Prince Charles, pointing to Mr. Bunny.

"No, for me," said Mrs. Bunny. "I mean, instead of queen."

"I'm afraid it's Dame and Sir or nothing," said Prince Charles apologetically.

"We'll take it," said Mr. Bunny, throwing Mrs. Bunny a look.

So Prince Charles picked up a letter opener from a nearby desk. "We usually use a sword, but I'm afraid your size, the weight and all—"

"Yes, yes, just get it over with. I like jam cakes too," said Mr. Bunny.

"Ixnay on the onetay," said Mrs. Bunny to Mr. Bunny. Didn't he know he was talking to a *prince*?

"By the power invested in me, I hereby pronounce you Sir and Dame Bunny," said Prince Charles.

"Is that really what you say? Isn't that what they use at wedding ceremonies?" asked Mrs. Bunny.

"Oh well, you know, specific words not so important, it's the intention. Now, how about a cup of tea and a jam cake? And I believe I'll go have a spot of gin."

"Yes, you do that," said Mr. Bunny. "Don't blame you a bit. It's what people often find they want after an encounter with Mrs. Bunny."

"Dame Bunny," hissed Mrs. Bunny. "Thank you—" she began, when she was interrupted by the majordomo, who had just come in.

"Sir," he said to Prince Charles, "might I escort you back to meet the foremost expert on ancient coins in Britain? Had to bring him in an armored vehicle. He won't leave the tent either. Seems he's afraid of squirrels."

The majordomo didn't notice the Bunnys, but Prince Charles bowed goodbye to them and tottered off to meet his other guests.

Mr. and Mrs. Bunny hopped back toward the tea tent.

"He *bowed* to us, Mr. Bunny."

"Hmm," said Mr. Bunny.

"And Mrs. Treaclebunny isn't anything. But *I'm* a dame," said Mrs. Bunny.

"Try to control yourself," said Mr. Bunny. "And please don't charge up to her and immediately start gloating or we won't be able to leave here until *she's* been made a dame and had the prince bow to *her.* All this royal muckety-muck has been fun, but now I've had enough."

Mrs. Bunny was busy wondering if being bowed to by a royal would have almost as much cachet among her hat clubbers as being *made* a royal. She decided it would. She hadn't heard anything Mr. Bunny had said, but she caught his tone.

"I don't know why you're complaining. You get to be Sir Bunny."

"You can use your title if you like, but I told you before, I am Mr. Bunny," said Mr. Bunny. "For so I am called. It's not the title that makes the bunny, it's the . . . ooooo, jam cakes!"

And Mr. Bunny hopped off like the wind and scooped up the last six. He clutched them in his greedy little paws. In the end he gave half to Mrs. Bunny. But it wasn't exactly his idea.

# MRS. BUNNY IS FINALLY CROWNED

The cruise home was mostly uneventful. Mr. Bunny got a first-class cabin for himself and Mrs. Bunny. Mrs. Bunny told Mrs. Treaclebunny that she would not answer unless addressed as Dame Bunny, so it was a very quiet journey home. This did not exactly break Mr. Bunny's heart.

Everyone was tired out from their adventures. Flo found a very good hiding place for the money they had made, and Mildred, now that she was aware what had happened to her shipboard, stayed in her cabin as much as possible in the lotus position, repeating to herself the mantra "I am not a fashionista. I am not a fashionista."

Mildred took all her meals in. For this reason she did not see the anomaly that intrigued Madeline and Katherine. Among all the finely dressed people at dinner was one family who sat alone every night at a table in the corner. They wore ragged clothes and looked tired and wary, their eyes darting one way, then the next. The girls could not imagine who they were.

One night while waltzing after dinner, the girls bumped into their old nemesis, Percy.

Madeline flinched and both girls prepared to run, as they felt he might justifiably hold them responsible for his involuntary stay in the infirmary. But before they could escape he said, "Now, now, all is forgiven and forgotten. Favor you did me, actually. Had to have sessions with the ship psychiatrist because they thought I was crazy. Wasn't crazy but had issues. You wouldn't believe how many."

"Yes, I would," said Madeline before she could stop herself.

"Fascinating thing, looking inward. Now that's all I do. No outward looking for me. Can I interest you girls in some insights?"

"Um," said Katherine.

"Actually," said Madeline, "we were just wondering who that family is over there. They're not in evening dress."

"Oh yes. Well, kind of bad luck they've had. They were supposed to immigrate but found out when they got to port that they didn't have enough money. No money, no relations, no job prospects. So they got turned down. And they can't go back where they came from. The captain is letting them live shipboard."

"You mean they just sail back and forth across the Atlantic?"

"Excellent man, our captain. Course, we all have issues," said Percy, and went off to do a little more soul searching and some light dusting.

Later when Madeline and Katherine went in to see Flo and Mildred and say good night, they told the story of the ragged family.

"Wow, heavy," said Flo. "Like, sad, Mildred, huh?"

"I am not a fashionista. I am not a fashionista," chanted Mildred.

"Wow. That's, like, so totally true," said Flo.

At last port was reached. It was September by now and the air had the tang of new beginnings. Mildred couldn't wait to get back and start clearing her new thirty acres and plotting out what kind of vegetables she would grow. Madeline and Katherine were excited about school.

"We'd better be in the same class!" said Madeline.

"No one would be so cruel as to keep us apart," agreed Katherine.

Mr. and Mrs. Bunny hugged the girls goodbye.

"And you can spend every weekend with us!" said Mr. Bunny.

"Mr. Bunny—" said Mrs. Bunny.

"And Thanksgiving. And Christmas!" said Mr. Bunny.

"We will see you as much as we can!" said Madeline.

"I'm going to try to learn Rabbit this winter!" said Katherine.

"That's lovely, dear," said Mrs. Bunny. "And I've got some knitting needles and patterns for both of you. In no time at all you'll find yourselves with enough floss to begin."

"Gee, thanks . . . ," said Madeline.

"And if you ask your friends to save their used dental floss for you, it will really speed up the process."

"Uh-huh," said Katherine.

"And if you get stuck on a pattern you can always come and visit and I'll help unstick you," said Mrs. Bunny.

"Or stuck on anything at all. We're always here. We'll always help. In fact, why bother going home at all . . . ," began Mr. Bunny.

Mrs. Bunny could see he was one hop away from trying to stuff the girls into the Smart car so she said, "Mr. Bunny, Mrs. Treaclebunny said she was taking a taxi but I think she's changed her mind. She seems to be hopping in this direction."

"Gotta go!" said Mr. Bunny. He gunned the engine and they were off, Mrs. Bunny wildly waving her dental floss hankie with one paw, the other pressed firmly over her eyes.

Madeline and Katherine ran to the taxi stand, where Mildred was already waiting in a cab. They all looked for Flo. He was back at the gangplank and appeared to be saying goodbye to the ragged family. They were bowing to him and he was bowing back. Back and forth and back and forth until Mildred shouted, "Hurry up, Flo!" He turned, spied them and ran to the taxi and off they headed for home.

First they dropped off Katherine in Comox. She and Madeline hugged goodbye among a volley of various kinds of balls and then Flo and Mildred and Madeline sped away to the ferry.

It was dinnertime when they finally reached Hornby. KatyD, who was one of the few people on the island with a car, came to pick them up and take them home. "Now, I gotta warn you, your place is . . . um, somewhat altered."

"What do you mean?" asked Mildred.

"Well, the campers kind of, um . . ." She didn't have to finish her sentence, for they had pulled into the driveway and Madeline and her parents saw for themselves. All Mildred's carefully tended land was in ruins. There was litter everywhere and small trees down. There were holes in the ground where people had dug campfire pits, and charred logs lay scattered everywhere.

"Oh dear," said Mildred.

"Yeah, sorry about that. I guess the campers were a little careless."

"Oh well," said Mildred in a small voice. "I suppose it will be a lot of work to bring it back, but I've got the thirty acres next door to work with too."

"Afraid not," said KatyD, clearing her throat. "I'm sure Zanky'll tell you herself when she sees you, but she's not selling. After she saw what the campers did to your place she started a whole new campaign to keep Hornby wild and untouched. She's trying to get a collective going to buy up more of Hornby for the land conservancy."

"But I was just going to grow veggies. Bring veggies to the people . . ." Mildred's voice trailed off.

"That was how we were going to make my college education money," said Madeline.

KatyD shrugged. "You know Zanky once she gets a bee in her bonnet. Well, welcome home. Your waitressing job is still available anytime you like, Madeline. There's still that."

Flo and Mildred and Madeline watched KatyD drive off

and then they collapsed in exhaustion on the front porch. The stars were coming out one by one, twinkling through the screen.

"It's good to be home," said Mildred. "It's hard to believe that I ever went into a shopping frenzy or dyed my hair blond."

"Or wanted me to go to Harvard just to be better than Ermintrude and Alfred," said Madeline.

"We must never leave the island," said Mildred. "That's what I realize now. I can only be Island Mildred here on Hornby. It is here I am my true self and walk in light and clarity."

"It's the vibe," agreed Flo.

"It's the goodness in the very soil," said Mildred, looking at her devastated garden again and sighing. "Well, anyhow, Zanky isn't the only one with thirty acres for sale. I'm sure we could buy a bit more land from someone else with our thirty thousand."

"If we had it," said Flo.

"Yes, if we . . . What?" said Mildred, sitting up. "What do you mean, IF?"

"I mean, man, that poor family had, like, nothing. Sailing back and forth."

"What poor family? You don't mean that immigrant family on the ship?" asked Mildred. "Was that what all that bowing was about when we were leaving? Were you *giving* them our money?"

"They were really grateful," said Flo. "But I said, man, it wasn't me. It was the universe. Go with the flow."

"How much did you give them?" asked Mildred.

"All of it, man."

"You gave them *ALL* our money?" said Mildred. "Without even asking us? The money that we needed for my garden? So we could bring veggies to the people and Madeline could go to college? What about the universe? Synchronicity? The confluence? Everything lining up for the one ultimate good?"

"Hey, man, don't you get it, that *was* the one ultimate good," said Flo. "Anyhow, anyone want a pistachio?" He opened his duffel and pulled out a bag.

Madeline and Mildred shook their heads.

"I, like, talked to that dad," said Flo in quieter tones between pistachios. "They had no home, no future, no way out. Those peops were scared. They got up every morning scared. They went to bed every night scared. You forget, like, how many people are just living in fear, man, living in fear."

Everyone sat in silence. After a while Madeline and Mildred accepted a few pistachios. They were hungry and that was all they had on hand for dinner. Normally in September they would have gone down to the garden and harvested something, but it would be a long time before they could do this again.

"Do we have *anything* left?" asked Madeline. "After you paid the cabdriver?"

"Let me see," said Flo, digging in his pockets and counting it up. "We've got six dollars and twenty-seven cents."

"Oh great," said Mildred. "That's *exactly* what we had before we started."

"What did I tell you, man," said Flo, happily cracking open another pistachio. "Synchronicity!"

The first day of school Mildred began cleaning up the land and preparing it for next year's garden. Flo began by making a shrine.

"What's that?" asked Madeline as she put on her old Salvation Army shoes and started down the driftwood-lined walkway to the ferry.

"The mystical Pop-Tart box that began it all," said Flo reverently as he placed the box in the center of the shrine. Madeline was about to tell him there was nothing at all mystical about the Pop-Tarts' arrival but she didn't have time to argue, she had to run to catch the ferry.

As she got to school Katherine pounced upon her with

tales of her own homecoming. Her brothers were all joining lacrosse this year.

"Do you know how much those balls hurt?" she asked indignantly. "Oh! And listen to this. My mother wrote Uncle Kevin to tell him not to send any more Pop-Tarts and guess what? He never sent them! And my mother never found out where they came from."

"It's a mystery," said Madeline. "Or maybe, like the candy, it's magical."

"Mr. Bunny would say that's magical *thinking*," said Katherine.

"Pshaw, he'd say," agreed Madeline.

"Maybe Flo was right about 'the mystical appearance of the Pop-Tarts'!" said Katherine.

"Uncle Runyon would say no one really knows how but it's all connected like the root system of aspen trees."

"And then someone would give him a grant to study it," said Katherine.

"Do you think we'll ever find out?" asked Madeline. "About the Pop-Tarts? About anything, really?"

"Maybe," said Katherine.

"Or maybe not," said Madeline.

"But maybe—" began Katherine.

She did not get a chance to finish her thought, for the first bell of the new school year rang, and this, with its promise of new beginnings, new teachers, fresh textbooks and always the chance of the unexpected, the unpredictable, the many things unknown and out of their control still to come, seemed rather magical to Madeline and Katherine too. They ran inside.

It was busy for the Bunnys when they got back. There was all that unpacking and laundry and sorting through the garden, which had grown like crazy. It wasn't even until several days had passed that Mrs. Treaclebunny came over to borrow something.

This time it was drill bits and farfel that Mrs. Bunny supplied. Mrs. Treaclebunny was hanging around with a handful of each at the front door. Mrs. Bunny was cleaning cupboards and not at all up to idle chitchat.

"So," said Mrs. Treaclebunny. "Tomorrow is the hat club meeting. Thought I'd tag along. Just heard about it. There was a notice on the bulletin board at the A&P."

"Oh," said Mrs. Bunny. She had an uneasy presentiment. She did not have presentiments often and she did not like it when she did.

"I'll be by at ten o'clock on my scooter to pick you up. We can go together."

"Uh-oh," said Mrs. Bunny to herself, and then she went back to her cupboards.

She had been looking forward to the hat club meeting. At what point should she announce that from now on she must be addressed as Dame Bunny? She had spent many mornings boring Mr. Bunny with this question. Later that afternoon she brought it up once again.

"Before refreshments or after? And I think I may tweak it. 'Dame and Sir Bunny' do not sound as fine as 'Lord and Lady Bunny' and I do not think North Americans know enough about titles to understand the Dame and Sir thing. 'Lord and Lady' rolls off the tongue much easier and sounds closer to royal titles. But when to tell them, Mr. Bunny? Maybe not around the refreshments, when they are focused on date squares. Maybe casually as people depart, as if it is no big deal."

"Why tell them at all? Why not let them suss it out on their own?" said Mr. Bunny.

"Suss it out on their . . . Oh really, Mr. Bunny. I don't know why I even ask you. You never take such things seriously."

"Oh yes, and be sure to tell the stirring tale of how you almost shot a fox but were too saintly," said Mr. Bunny, evilly smiling into his handkerchief while pretending to blow his nose.

"Hmm, I believe I will save that for the second meeting,"

said Mrs. Bunny, and returned to the problem of when to tell them she was now almost royalty. It was such a special announcement, almost like the time she got to announce that she had made over, entirely out of lint, her and Mr. Bunny's bedroom ceiling to look just like the Sistine Chapel! She had planned that announcement for days so that it fell at an auspicious part of the meeting when there would be optimum clapping. Yes, optimum clapping was the thing.

When Mrs. Treaclebunny picked up Mrs. Bunny on her scooter, Mrs. Bunny was once again mulling over the timing of her announcement. She was still trying to decide later at the meeting as she dutifully introduced Mrs. Treaclebunny about. Then Mrs. Treaclebunny went off on her own. She needed very little encouragement to chatter nonstop to whoever fell in her way. By midmeeting Mrs. Bunny started to hear some whispered comments.

"She isn't going to come *every* week, is she?" asked Mrs. Binglybunny.

"Oh, my fur and whiskers, if she told us about her duchess relative once, she told us a dozen times," said Mrs. Hushbunny.

"Have you ever seen such social climbing?" asked Mrs. Butterballbunny.

"Have you ever seen such name-dropping?" agreed Mrs. Sneepbunny.

"As if we here in Canada *care* about such things as titles."

"Too full of herself. Is there some way to *un*invite her to join our club?" asked Mrs. Snowbunny.

"You must ask Mrs. Bunny to do it. She's the one who invited her," said Mrs. Ruskeebunny.

And so after refreshments Mrs. Bunny, instead of announcing she was Lady Bunny, as she had been looking forward to for so long, was given the very unpleasant job of sometime in the near future uninviting Mrs. Treaclebunny.

She was very quiet the rest of the meeting.

But not so Mrs. Treaclebunny on the ride home.

"Kind of a bunch of stiffs, those bunnies," she said to Mrs. Bunny. "Didn't even know what a *Yang di-Pertuan Agong* is. Jeez, don't get out much, do they? Course, I suppose I raised the tone of the meeting somewhat. But raising the tone is hard work. Hard work. Hard, hard, hard. Well, here you are at home. See ya later, alligator!"

Mrs. Bunny climbed wearily off the scooter and Mrs. Treaclebunny zipped on up her own driveway.

Inside, Mr. Bunny picked up on Mrs. Bunny's mood in a trice.

"Well," he said. "Were they duly impressed with Your Lady-ship?"

"Oh, Mr. Bunny," said Mrs. Bunny, rushing to her favorite chair and collapsing in it with her head on her knees and her paws over her eyes. "We must never, never, never tell people about our titles."

"Well, I won't if you won't," said Mr. Bunny cheerily.

"Mrs. Treaclebunny *would* go on and on about being related to a duchess and now she is *shunned*."

"You don't say," said Mr. Bunny with great unconcern, turning the pages of his newspaper. "Well, well. Shame." He smiled. He could not help it. But then when Mrs. Bunny did not lift her head for seventeen minutes and was silent all through lunch, he began to worry. Mrs. Bunny was not a glum bunny. It was not in her nature. And she *had* been looking forward for days to telling her hat-clubbing friends about her title. It was a small-enough pleasure. Now turned to dust. Mr. Bunny began to feel sadder and sadder. His whiskers drooped. He did not like Mrs. Bunny in such a state. *He* was supposed to be the glum one. It was supposed to be *her* job to cheer *him* up. Suppose she was too depressed to make carrot cakes? Something must be done. He hopped into the Smart car and drove to town.

When Mr. Bunny returned he secreted a package in the buffet, then found Mrs. Bunny and said experimentally, "Good cake-baking weather."

Later that afternoon Mrs. Bunny perked up somewhat when a letter from Madeline arrived. She and Mr. Bunny sat out in the garden enjoying the September sunshine, eating carrot cake and reading and rereading Madeline's letter to each other.

"This is tragic! No money to buy land," said Mrs. Bunny.

"And Zanky closed down the campground before they made any more money on that. So they are back to square one, tsk tsk," said Mr. Bunny.

"Oh, poor, poor Madeline!"

"Well, at least Mildred is looking for ways to make money to buy land. It has at least taught Mildred and Flo—well, Mildred, anyhow—to plan ahead. Perhaps they will even give Madeline's college fund a passing thought."

"The organic farm does seem the most foresighted idea," said Mrs. Bunny.

"Yes, to invest in an organic veggie garden that will keep making money."

"Organic vegetables are *very* expensive," said Mrs. Bunny, who, when their own veggie garden gave out, bought her carrots at the A&P, eschewing the organics for the more reasonably priced carrots. Mr. Bunny would have quite the conniption if she spent an extra two dollars just because it said *organic* on the bag.

"After all," he often said. "Organic carrots are just carrots, Mrs. Bunny, they are not made of gold."

"And speaking of gold," said Mrs. Bunny as these thoughts ran through her head.

"I don't believe we were," said Mr. Bunny.

"Well, in my head you were," said Mrs. Bunny.

"Please do not take us on any little treks into the deeper recesses of your head, Mrs. Bunny," said Mr. Bunny. He was feeling expansive and happy now that he was back in his own hutch. He stretched his short little bunny legs out in front of him and basked in the sunshine and a third piece of carrot cake.

"If you would only get busy and figure out a way to convert the carrot standard to the gold standard, we could start a bank account for Madeline ourselves."

"Yes, I will take it up with the Bunny Council," said Mr. Bunny.

"Oh!" said Mrs. Bunny, putting her paws over her eyes. "Do you dare? They are so fierce!"

"Ha! They are no match for Mr. Bunny. I should have been

a lawyer. My arguing skills are paramount. Nobody knows as many long confusing words as Mr. Bunny. I dazzle. And speaking of professions, we already have one. We are writers."

"Writers usually need more than one profession," said Mrs. Bunny gloomily. "If they are to make anything resembling a living." Then she paused. "And what do you mean by 'we'?"

"I am glad you have asked, Mrs. Bunny," said Mr. Bunny, pulling out his notebook, where he had kept track of their trip expenses and also written his own bunny writing notes. He passed it over and let Mrs. Bunny read the bit he had written on the way to Stratford. He watched Mrs. Bunny's face. He did not like the way her ears twitched.

"Hmmm," said Mrs. Bunny when she was done. "It seems to me that it owes a lot to that favorite sitcom of yours. These bits are very like some they do on that show."

"Yes, that is just what is so funny!" said Mr. Bunny, clawing at his fur in frustration.

"What, stealing someone's bits is funny?"

"Yes, exactly. That's the joke!"

"You mean like an homage?"

"No, I mean . . . oh, never mind," said Mr. Bunny. "You are determined to be deliberately obtuse."

"And I object to Mrs. Bunny saying 'Can it, marmotbreath!' Mrs. Bunny would never use language like that."

"It would be funnier if she did," said Mr. Bunny.

"Are you sure you want me to insert this in the manuscript?" asked Mrs. Bunny, thinking, oh well, she could let Mr. Bunny duke it out with the editor.

"Yes, and the chapter titles. You said I could make them this time."

"I said we could both make them and let the reader pick."

"Yes, but after reading the manuscript I have decided yours are pooey, so I have already scratched them out," said Mr. Bunny. "And I want a credit this time on the cover. And my own bio. How else is the world to know that Mr. Bunny was once a marmot wrangler?"

"Right," said Mrs. Bunny, nervously shoving cake into her mouth. She wasn't so sure she wanted a coauthor anymore. She was trying to figure out how to broach this subject in a tactful way when the thought of a coauthor triggered a new idea. "MR. BUNNY! I nearly forgot. We have a bank account already on the gold standard!" And she told him about the money the translator had put aside for her.

"I cannot believe you forgot to tell me about a bank account," said Mr. Bunny.

"Never mind that now. You know I've had a lot of queenship thingies on my mind."

"But I see where you are going with this, Mrs. Bunny. I

must figure out how to convert that money from the gold standard to the carrot standard and then we can convert it to the gold standard again to put it into an account for Madeline! She will have her college fund after all. All ends happily."

"And synchronistically."

"You promised never to use that word again."

"Didn't. By the way, wouldn't it be easier just to leave it unconverted and on the gold standard to begin with?" asked Mrs. Bunny.

"Mrs. Bunny, you always take the easy way out."

"I do not. That is a privilege left to queens!" And Mrs. Bunny began to look sad again.

"Oh, PLEEEEEASE, don't sniffle. It's really getting on my nerves! Look at what Mr. Bunny got you!" Mr. Bunny leapt up, led Mrs. Bunny inside, and took a box out of the drawer of the buffet.

"What's that?" asked Mrs. Bunny. Could it be a present? Mrs. Bunny did so love presents.

"Because I know that with you, Mrs. Bunny, it is always about the hats, I bought you this. I am sorry that you cannot be Lady Bunny at the hat club. I know how much you were looking forward to that. And I am very sorry you cannot be queen," he said, crossing his fingers behind his back. "But you will always be queen of my heart."

Mrs. Bunny thought that Mr. Bunny's speeches were always very nice at the start until he veered into the overly flowery. But she regretted this momentary small-mindedness, for when she opened the box, there sat a magnificent rhinestone tiara.

"You see," said Mr. Bunny, putting it on her head, "it is your own crown. I suggest you wear it only around the house."

"Oh, Mr. Bunny, this is so kind of you," said Mrs. Bunny.

"Yes, it is, rather . . . ," began Mr. Bunny, when there was a knock on the door and who should hop in but Mrs. Treaclebunny.

"Bunch of stiffs at that club of yours. The more I think about it, the more stiffedy they seem to me," she said, coming in and plopping herself in Mr. Bunny's chair. "And their refreshments are not of the best carroty sort. So, after much thought, I don't believe I'll be going there again."

Mrs. Bunny sighed in relief. She would not have to tell Mrs. Treaclebunny she was being shunned. Mrs. Treaclebunny was doing proactive shunning. Good for her!

"Hey, what's that on your head?" asked Mrs. Treaclebunny, peering suspiciously.

"Within these walls, as you can see," said Mr. Bunny, "Mrs. Bunny is queen."

"Humph," said Mrs. Treaclebunny, arising and hopping swiftly out the door.

"Well, it seems we have finally found out how to get rid of her," said Mr. Bunny.

"Oh, the poor thing," said Mrs. Bunny. "She has had such a miserable day. Even if she doesn't know it."

"Brought it on herself," said Mr. Bunny, and opened his paper.

He was reading bits to Mrs. Bunny about the new cabbage tariff as she sat and knit in a queenly fashion when in bounced Mrs. Treaclebunny without even knocking this time. On her head was a rhinestone tiara. Twice the size of Mrs. Bunny's.

"HA!" said Mrs. Treaclebunny. "I said to myself, where would Mr. Bunny find a tiara? And I was right. On sale this week at Bunny-Mart. Half-price. So we are back where we started. You are the subqueen. And I am the queen."

And she pulled up a chair from the kitchen and sat next to Mrs. Bunny. Then she placed a phone book on her chair so that she sat a bit taller than Mrs. Bunny.

"Am not the subqueen," muttered Mrs. Bunny sulkily.

"Are so," said Mrs. Treaclebunny. "Are so, are so, are so."

"Oh, all right," said Mrs. Bunny.

They sat there for an hour with Mr. Bunny reading, Mrs. Bunny knitting and Mrs. Treaclebunny staring grumpily at the wall until her ears got tired from holding on to the tiara. It did not fit quite properly. She had chosen it because it was so very large. Mr. Bunny had more wisely chosen for Mrs. Bunny a small one that could be maintained without a lot of ear support. When Mrs. Treaclebunny's ears were on the verge of giving out, she got up and very carefully hopped out the door and home. She had wanted them to say "Good Night, Your Majesty," but Mr. Bunny made a sound that Mrs. Treaclebunny had never heard before and she decided not to press her luck.

"Why do you let people do that?" Mr. Bunny asked Mrs. Bunny when Mrs. Treaclebunny had left. "Why do you let them hop all over you? You didn't have to let her be queen. She already has an ocean view."

"Yes, Mr. Bunny, but I have *you,*" said Mrs. Bunny.

"True, too true," said Mr. Bunny. "Sometimes, Mrs. Bunny, you get it just right."

And he went whistling up to bed.

"Darn tootin'," said Mrs. Bunny, getting out the manuscript, crossing out all of Mr. Bunny's chapter titles and replacing them with her own. She sealed the envelope and addressed it to Bunny Publishing. Then, feeling much better about the world in general and deciding the next hat club meeting was not too soon to let it somehow drop that Prince Charles had *bowed* to her, she too went whistling up to bed.